Curious George®

The Movie

The Movie

A Junior Novel

Adapted by Kathleen W. Zoehfeld

Based on the motion picture story by Ken Kaufman

Motion picture screenplay by Ken Kaufman and David Reynolds

Based on the books by Margret and H. A. Rey

Houghton Mifflin Company, Boston 2005

www.houghtonmifflinbooks.com

The text of this book is set in AGaramond.
Book design by Joyce White
Composition by Pamela A. Consolazio

ISBN-13: 978-0618-60591-0

Manufactured in the United States of America
QUM 10 9 8 7 6 5 4 3 2 1

Curious George®
The Movie

CONTENTS

A Curious Monkey's Day

One beautiful morning in Africa, a curious little monkey crouched on a lily pad in the middle of a wide blue lake. He was busy making funny faces at his reflection in the water when something silvery caught his eye. Bubbles! He poked one with his finger and . . . POP!

What could be making such interesting bubbles? The monkey wanted to know so he took a deep breath and dove in. There, on the bottom of the lake, he saw a mother hippo, sound asleep next to her hippo baby. The bigger hippo snored contentedly. A hippo nose — that's what was making the bubbles!

The curious little monkey was eager to play. He reached out and covered one nostril on the sleeping hippo. Only half as many bubbles rose to the surface now. Then he covered the other nostril. The bubbles stopped completely.

The startled hippo rushed to the surface, gasping for air. The

much smaller monkey was caught in her wake and surfaced too. The mother hippo wasted no time in chasing him ashore.

The baby hippo watched and giggled. What a funny monkey!

On his way out of the water, the still-curious little monkey noticed an egg lying in the mud. It was all by itself. He picked it up and looked around. Being a monkey, he was a very good climber, and he had no trouble carrying the egg all the way up to a bird's nest high in the branches of a nearby tree. The monkey carefully set the egg next to the two smaller eggs already there. Looking at the eggs neatly tucked into the nest, he wondered what it would be like to be a mama bird. He decided to try it.

"Squawk!" The mother bird had arrived, and she wasted no time in kicking the little monkey out of her nest. But just then the eggs began to hatch, and the little monkey lingered to watch. Wow, what a big baby was hatching out of the egg he'd just rescued. The monkey had never seen a baby bird with sharp, snapping teeth, scaly skin, and a long tail. Neither had the mother bird, for that matter. She pushed the strange hatchling right out of the nest!

Quickly the little monkey scampered down the tree and caught the scaly baby in midair. He set it back on the muddy bank where he'd found it in the first place. Yikes! A much bigger,

scarier version of the baby lunged and snapped at him. The monkey escaped into the tall grass, just ahead of a very angry crocodile mom.

Deciding it was safe now, the monkey slowed down as he came to a clearing. He took a deep breath and discovered that a blade of grass had gotten stuck to his lips. He tried to blow it away. *Thweep!* That was a funny sound! Had the grass made that sound? The monkey blew again. *Thweep!* It *was* the grass.

Just then the monkey spied a pride of lions dozing beside a water hole. The monkey was too curious to be afraid. He tiptoed up to the sleeping lions. He carefully placed a single blade of grass in each lion's mouth. Soon the lions' snoring had turned into a symphony of thweeping. The monkey smiled.

One of the lions woke up. The monkey good-naturedly thweeped at him with his own grass horn.

"Raaarrrrrrr!" growled the angry cat.

Realizing that he had better be quick, the nimble monkey bolted away through the long yellow grass.

In short time the monkey was among trees again. He passed a chameleon. The monkey was startled to see that the animal had turned brown to match his monkey fur. How interesting! The monkey had an idea.

He brought back a baby rhino. When the little gray rhino came close to the chameleon, the lizard turned from brown to gray. Next the monkey tried a flamingo. The lizard turned pink. The monkey wondered if the chameleon would become striped next to a zebra baby. Yes, he would!

The excited monkey led all the young animals he'd collected in a dance around the chameleon. Around and around they went. All the while the chameleon changed from pink to gray to brown . . . to striped . . . to polka dotted . . . to pink again, trying to keep up with the animal procession until finally, at last, the poor confused lizard keeled over, exhausted. Oh, my! Chittering in concern, the monkey set the multicolored chameleon on a branch to rest.

Next the little monkey climbed up through the jungle canopy, following a beautiful butterfly. He jumped on a branch and *plop!* — a pomegranate fell on his head. He tasted the delicious fruit. Soon the monkey's hands were covered with red juice. He jumped down from his perch and wiped his vivid red hands on a rock. Interesting . . . He liked the look of his handprint, so he thought he'd make more on different rocks. Suddenly one of the rocks giggled. It was a baby elephant!

The other little animals saw what had happened and wanted

to get in on the fun. They eagerly lined up to have their faces painted. One . . . two . . . three . . . the monkey went down the line, using the zebra's tail as a paintbrush. Oops! Before he knew it, a mama elephant had stepped into the line and he'd accidentally painted her leg. She scowled at the naughty little monkey and trumpeted for the other animal parents to come and take their babies home.

The grownups huffed and harrumphed at the monkey as they led their children away. Left alone once again, the poor monkey sighed. No one understood that he just wanted to have fun. No one understood that he was just curious.

As the sun began to set, he climbed one of his favorite trees and gave it a good shake. He watched the dry leaves drift gently to the ground. He climbed down and fluffed the leaves into a nice soft bed, just as he always did, and curled up to sleep.

A Visit to the Oswald J. Bloomsberry Natural History Museum

Across an ocean and far away, in a big city near the water, the day was just beginning. Every Thursday, come rain or shine, Miss Maggie Dunlop's class took their regular field trip to the Oswald J. Bloomsberry Natural History Museum. Maggie made sure they arrived bright and early. On this particular Thursday, as they climbed the marble stairs toward the grand Corinthian columns that framed the entryway, they caught a glimpse of Ted, the museum curator, turning on the lights inside.

Ted smiled to himself with pleasure at the familiar displays: the whale hanging from the ceiling, the huge dinosaur skeleton, the dioramas of different animals in their wild habitats, and the scenes of ancient peoples going about their daily lives.

Ted gathered his lecture notes and stood proudly beside the caveman diorama, while Maggie's class filed in.

"Life was a constant struggle for survival," he began once they had settled down. "*Australopithecus* had no time to enjoy himself because around every corner was danger."

He flung an arm out in a dramatic gesture and knocked the head off one of the wax cavemen.

"Oh, good one" and "Way to go," the kids called out. A few were already staring off into space, or about to fall asleep.

Oblivious to the sea of blank faces before him, Ted droned on: "As we all know, it wasn't until *Homo erectus* that man was able to take time and enjoy life. Why was that?" He pointed at the wax cave dwellers. "What made Ogg and Grogg's life so much better?"

The kids shouted out silly answers.

"The Internet?"

"Video games!"

"A rocket sled?"

"Um . . . that wasn't a real question," said Ted.

"Secret pirate treasure?"

"A mountain of chocolate!"

Ted plowed on bravely, lifting his voice one decibel louder

than the children: "That's right, *fire!*" He lit a match for realistic effect. The kids held their breath and watched his hands.

"Oooh. Aaah. Look at that! Impressive!" he gushed.

"Ms. Dunlop," whispered one of the kids, "why do we come to this boring museum every week?"

But Maggie thought Ted was wonderful. "It's not boring; it's very interesting," she insisted.

"Ow, ow, ow!" Ted cried as the match began to burn his fingers.

"Oh, no," gasped Maggie.

"Ooh, hot, fire's hot." Ted juggled his flaming note cards. He dropped them to the floor and stamped out the fire.

"Um, where was I?" he mumbled.

"Is that a real spear?" asked one of the kids out of the blue.

"Can we play with it?" asked another.

"Kids, a museum is a place where we *observe* — we don't *play,*" said Ted.

"Well, what else can we do?"

"Yeah, this is *boring,*" whined the kids.

"If you want to go on a *real* adventure, I have just the thing — A TIME MACHINE!"

The kids perked up. "A time machine?" "No way!" "Cooool!" They all shouted for joy.

"A time machine called" — Ted paused dramatically — "My Imagination! Where knowledge is my engine and books are my fuel. Who wants to come with me?"

The kids exchanged looks of dread.

"Oh, dear," muttered Maggie.

"Come on!" Ted cajoled. "Plenty of room in Ted's time machine. Get your tickets stamped. All aboard!"

"Lunchtime!" cried one inspired kid.

"Yeah! Lunch!" Everyone cheered.

"It's only nine a.m.," said Ted.

Moving by instinct, the herd stampeded away toward the cafeteria, leaving Ted and Maggie standing alone by the diorama.

"Buddy system! Stay with your buddies!" Maggie called as her class vanished down the hall.

Ted looked slightly perplexed.

"Oh, each kid has a buddy so they can all keep track of each other," explained Maggie. She looked into his eyes sweetly. "Everyone needs a partner, right?"

"Yeah . . . I guess." Ted hesitated, looking more perplexed. "I'm not following you. . . ."

"Um . . . well," Maggie began, unsure. The two stared at each other for a moment.

Suddenly Ted's face brightened. "Lungfish!" he exclaimed.

"Excuse me?"

"Next Thursday," declared Ted. "I'm going to talk to your class about lungfish."

"Oh," said Maggie.

"It should be pretty wild," he gushed. "The lungfish is believed to be the closest living relative of the first tetrapods."

"I look forward to hearing about it," said Maggie.

"It is pretty great," said Ted.

"You know, I look forward to all your Thursday lectures," said Maggie. "I wish today was Thursday. . . ." She bumped into one of the chrome poles that held the velvet ropes cordoning off the cave exhibit.

They both scrambled awkwardly to catch it, but it clattered to the floor.

"Well . . . I know it *is* Thursday," she said, flustered, "but when it's not . . . I wish it was."

"Don't worry. It's not a big deal," said Ted about the pole. They both reached for it and his hand brushed against hers. . . .

Maggie drew her hand back shyly. She could hear her kids yelling in the cafeteria. "I should go catch up with my lungfish — I, uh, I mean, class."

"Way to go, Maggie," she whispered to herself as she hurried down the hall.

"I'll see you next week, Ms. Dunlop," called Ted.

It was time to begin his daily routine. He adjusted the cavemen, tidied up the moss, and rearranged the rocks. He had been working for only a few minutes when he heard the museum's director, Oswald J. Bloomsberry, calling his name. He looked up from the exhibit. "Mr. Bloomsberry!"

"Walk with me, Ted," the older man said.

As they strolled past the dioramas, Mr. Bloomsberry shook his head sadly. "I'm afraid that Ogg and Grogg — *all* our friends here . . . they're not the attractions they used to be."

"What do you mean?" asked Ted.

Mr. Bloomsberry put his arm around his favorite curator. "It breaks my heart, but I have to sell the museum. We're broke."

"Broke?" cried Ted. "But — Mr. Bloomsberry, the museum *can't* close!"

The Lost Shrine of Zagawa

Mr. Bloomsberry led Ted into his office. Ted had always loved this warm, wood-paneled place. It was full of old photos, African spears, strange fossils, and shrunken heads. But he hated to listen now to the sad facts Mr. Bloomsberry had to relate.

"I have no choice, Ted," he continued. "Museum attendance is down. No one's buying anything from the gift shop. . . ."

"Not even the glow-in-the-dark star stickers?" asked Ted.

"Not even the glow-in-the-dark star stickers," Mr. Bloomsberry said.

"Man, I love those," Ted admitted, forgetting the bad news for a moment. "I especially love the Milky Way and . . . oh, wait. What'll happen to the museum?"

Mr. Bloomsberry went to the fireplace and stoked the fire with his metal-tipped cane. The old bones in his back creaked.

"I'm glad you asked," crowed a voice much like Mr. Bloomsberry's, but younger. Mr. Bloomsberry's office chair spun around to reveal — Bloomsberry junior! Mr. Bloomsberry's son held out a small-scale replica of the museum.

"It will be gutted and a parking lot put in its place. With high hourly rates and no daily maximums. Ka-ching!" Junior delighted in making a noise like a cash register.

He popped the roof off the model museum and Ted peered in. The interior had been redesigned as a parking garage, filled with toy cars.

"The world doesn't need another parking lot!" cried Ted. "The world needs a place where kids' brains can grow."

"Exactly," declared Junior. "That's why I'm thinking they can grow while trying to count all the spaces in the new parking lot. C'mon, how fun is that?"

Ted moaned. "He's not serious, is he?"

"It's time to sell, Father," said Junior. "We're not going to get a better offer."

"I know, I know." Mr. Bloomsberry sighed.

"Wait!" cried Ted. "What if we did something?"

Mr. Bloomsberry gave him a questioning glance.

"Aaahhh . . . uh . . . something crazy!"

Mr. Bloomsberry's face brightened.

"What if we got an amazing new exhibit?" suggested Ted, excited.

Junior rolled his eyes and sipped his coffee. "You know, Ted, you need to worry about finding an amazing new job."

But Mr. Bloomsberry wanted to hear Ted out. "Well, hold on, Junior."

Junior rose indignantly and sloshed his coffee all over Mr. Bloomsberry's desk. "Oh, great."

"Ted," said Mr. Bloomsberry, "if you have an idea, now is the time to speak up. What exhibit?"

"Yes," echoed Junior, "what exhibit?" He went over to the bulletin board and unpinned some old papers to wipe up the spilled coffee.

"Uh, it's the . . . famous . . ." Ted began.

"Uh-huh . . . ?" said Junior skeptically.

"And . . ." Ted racked his brains for an idea.

"Yes?" asked Mr. Bloomsberry.

"And rare, of course . . ."

"Yes."

"The incredible . . ."

"Come on," Mr. Bloomsberry encouraged him.

"Spit it out," said Junior.

Ted scanned the room desperately for inspiration. Something on the bulletin board caught his eye. When Junior had removed those papers, he had unknowingly uncovered an old poster describing a mysterious monkey shrine.

"What about the Lost Shrine of Zagawa?" cried Ted.

Mr. Bloomsberry had not thought of the legend in years. "My goodness," he said, stunned.

"The — I'm sorry — the lost . . . ? You lost me at 'the lost,' " said Junior.

"The Lost Shrine of Zagawa," repeated Mr. Bloomsberry. "It's an ancient idol." He hobbled to his bookcase and took down an old leatherbound journal. He blew the dust off its covers and flipped nostalgically through the pages of notes and maps. "Twenty tons of granite carved by a thousand craftsmen over a hundred years. I had all the charts ready. I was prepared to go to Africa when . . . something happened. It slips my mind. . . ."

"Hello, how about the birth of your only son?" Junior reminded him. "That would be me."

"Ah, yes. Then I began another adventure — raising Junior."

"Well, now that that's done —" said Ted, grabbing a pith helmet and putting it on the old man's head, "you can finally finish what you've started." He pulled the poster down off the bulletin board and presented it to Mr. Bloomsberry with a dramatic flourish. "Which is bringing home —"

"The Lost Shrine of Zagawa!" cheered Bloomsberry.

"You'll put this museum on the map!" cried Ted.

"I'll need a team of ten men," declared Bloomsberry.

"At least ten men," agreed Ted.

"It's a four-day hike into the jungle."

Ted hung a pair of binoculars around the old man's neck.

Bloomsberry climbed onto his desk and stood proudly, as if he had just scaled Mount Kilimanjaro. "We'll be cutting through heavy brush for twelve hours a day."

Ted put a machete in his gnarled hand. "Look out! Here comes the Bloomsberry Express!" he cheered.

"Yes! Yes!" cried Mr. Bloomsberry, posing heroically.

"Next stop: archeological fame and fortune!" shouted Ted.

Bloomsberry swung his machete. "I'm going to Africa to discover the Lost Shrine of Zagawaaaaaaaa. . . ." The weight of the big knife threw Bloomsberry off balance and he toppled off the desk, landing with a thump in his chair.

"Owwww," he moaned. "I forgot something — I'm really old."

Junior tapped the parking-lot contract with his pen. "Okay, can I have the Bloomsberry Express pull into the Reality Station and sign here?"

"Wait!" cried Ted. "I guess *I* could go.

"Did I just say that? I can't do that. I don't even ride the bus. Maybe they didn't hear me." Ted shook his head. "I'm sorry, sir, you were saying?"

"Excellent idea, Ted!" cried Mr. Bloomsberry.

"He did hear me," muttered Ted.

"Him?" cried Junior. "You've got to be kidding me. Ted is not an explorer."

"He raises a good point," said Ted.

Mr. Bloomsberry handed Ted the pith helmet. "Nonsense! With my maps and my journal, a six-year-old could find that shrine."

"Thank you," said Ted. "I think."

Bloomsberry threw his arm around Ted's shoulders and led him out of the office.

"Come on. Let's get ready for your big adventure," said Mr. Bloomsberry. " . . . Now Ted, the journal won't take you right to the idol."

"It won't?" Ted asked.

"No, you have to use your instincts," said Mr. Bloomsberry.

"Sir, I believe I misspoke. . . ."

"Don't worry," Mr. Bloomsberry said cheerfully. "It will be fun."

Junior lingered behind and waited until they had disappeared around the corner. He scowled at the two photographs hanging over his father's mantel: one of his dad and Ted together, arm in arm; the other of himself, alone. "Why does my father like you best?" he asked the photo of Ted. "It's not fair — I've got the ponytail."

He grabbed his father's journal and flipped to the last page. An "X" marked the spot on the map where the shrine stood. Junior tore out the last two pages of the journal and made an "X" on the new last page instead.

"Sorry, Ted, but that's as close as you're ever going to get to your precious Lost Shrine of Zagaga-wawa," he mocked as he crumpled up the pages and tossed them into the fire.

The Man in the Yellow Hat

Ted peered into the display window of the fanciest safari outfitters in the city. An impressive mannequin, dressed from head to toe in explorer's gear and holding a whip in its hand, stared vacantly out toward him. Ted could see his own face reflected in the glass, and he moved until his worried visage fit exactly over the mannequin's blank one.

So that's what I look like as a great jungle explorer, thought Ted, trying to build up his courage. Okay, the trick is to look like you know what you're doing.

While the "great explorer" figured out how to find the front door, two salespeople were busy arranging the racks of clothing inside.

"Yellow? Six dozen yellow suits," counted the store manager. "Tony, what are ya — goofy? We can't sell these things."

The man named Tony shrugged. "If the big guy says move 'em, we move 'em."

"Yeah, sure, but what kind of meatball would buy these?"

"Ah, excuse me. . . ." A timid voice interrupted their conversation. They looked up, and there was Ted standing in the doorway.

"I'm here to be professionally outfitted for a jungle expedition," declared Ted.

The salesmen sized Ted up immediately. Here was just the ignoramus they were hoping for. The manager shifted smoothly into his most convincing Australian outback accent. "G'day, mate! You've stepped into the right place! Isn't that right, Nigel?"

"I'll say it is, Steve-o!" replied Tony. "Finally, a real adventurer to suit up."

The salesmen hustled Ted to the dressing room and brought him a pile of safari clothes to try on — all of them yellow.

"How does the suit fit, mate?" asked the manager.

"It . . . it fits well," said Ted hesitantly. "I . . . I'm just not so sure about the color."

Ted stepped out of the dressing room looking like a glowing neon school bus. He checked himself out in the three-way mirror. "Isn't the idea to try to *blend into* the jungle?" he asked.

"All the adventurers wear yellow now," said the manager.

"Not khaki?" asked Ted.

"Yellow's the new khaki," declared the manager.

"Yeah, that's right. New khaki, mate," agreed Tony.

"Really? Well okay!" said Ted.

The next day peals of laughter greeted Ted as he boarded the ship to Africa dressed in his new yellow safari outfit. Everyone else — all the *real* adventurers — were wearing khaki.

"Well, *you* fit right in," joked one of the other explorers on board.

Ted realized he'd been had. "The new khaki indeed," he muttered. "Thank you!" he shouted at the air as the boat left the dock. "Thank you very much! I look like an idiot!"

Finding the Shrine

With his nose buried in Mr. Bloomsberry's journal, a yellow-clad Ted led a line of African porters carrying supplies through the jungle. Edu, the head porter, walked beside him.

"Edu, this expedition we're on — we only have one shot," fretted Ted. "And we cannot deviate from this journal."

In a nearby part of the jungle, a curious little monkey was decorating a spider web with leaves. He placed them carefully. The spider next to him snickered at the smiley face design.

The monkey was distracted by a herd of elephants passing by. They trumpeted loudly. Eager to join them, the little monkey hitched a ride on a baby elephant's tail. But his mother wasn't very happy about it. She shooed the mischievous monkey away.

As Ted's expedition approached a sunny clearing, the porters noticed some colorful monkey handprints on the rocks. "Hey, look at that! Wow. That's beautiful," they all exclaimed.

"Edu, do you see *this?*" asked Ted.

"Yes," said Edu, admiring one of the handprints.

"It's exciting. We are so close," said Ted.

Edu frowned. He realized Ted was talking about his journal, not the art.

"This way, men," ordered Ted. He led them into a cluster of bushes. When he finally looked up from his book, it was just in time to see more of the talented monkey's handiwork — a big rock rhino.

"A rhino!" he cried. He pulled the tranquilizer gun out of his pack and aimed. "Stand aside, men! I'm just going to put him to sleep!"

"Sir," cried Edu, "that's not a rhino. . . ."

Everyone ducked for cover as Ted fired the dart. *Ping!* It ricocheted off the rock and jabbed poor Edu in the neck.

"Nice shot, Mr. Ted," he moaned, tipping over slowly like a tree.

Ted studied Edu's fallen bulk. "Okay, let's break for lunch," he told the porters, "— for the next four to six hours, or longer, depending on how much he weighs."

On a branch overhead, the curious monkey was stopping for his lunch too. The monkey peeled a banana. He was about to take a bite when he spotted something interesting: a giant yellow banana bouncing along atop a row of bushes! The monkey looked at his own small banana in dismay and tossed it away.

Ted sat down on a fallen log and continued to study Bloomsberry's maps, with a sandwich by his side.

"Hmmm, we're close." He grunted and reached for his sandwich. He was about to take a bite when *swoosh!* — his hat flew right off his head.

"Huh?"

Crunch! The hungry monkey tried to take a bite of the giant "banana."

Ted spotted the little hat-snatcher up in the tree. "Oh, a monkey. Hey there, little guy. Can I have my hat please? Sun's hot and I freckle. Actually, I blotch. So please, my hat?"

The monkey held the hat out.

"Yes, that's the one," Ted coaxed.

But the monkey pulled it back. Ted sighed and scratched his head, trying to figure out what to do next.

The monkey sighed and scratched his head the same way.

Hmmm, thought Ted. He mimed putting an imaginary hat on his head.

The monkey put the real hat on.

Then Ted mimed a throwing action.

The monkey tossed the hat and caught it with one of his feet.

"That's not fair!" cried Ted. "You have four hands."

The monkey jumped down from the branch, using the hat as a parachute. The hat came down on top of him, covering him completely.

"Hello. Anybody in there?" asked Ted. He lifted up one edge of the hat. "Peekaboo!"

The monkey grinned.

Ted let the hat down, then lifted it again. "Peekaboo!"

The monkey giggled.

"Peekaboo!" Ted lifted the hat off completely.

"Look at that," he said, gazing at the monkey fondly. "A monkey who likes to play peekaboo." He patted the monkey on the head and put his hat back on.

"Well, this was fun, but sorry, my little friend. I gotta go." Ted walked away and . . .

FWOOP! The yellow hat vanished from his head and ran away through the jungle on monkey legs.

"Hey!" he cried. "Come back here!"

The monkey ducked behind a tree. Ted chased him. Around and around the tree they went.

Finally the monkey hopped away from the tree and watched, amused, as Ted kept circling.

"That's right. I can run all night! All day and all night!" Ted cried. "There's nothing that can stop — ow!" Ted stopped and began hopping on one foot. "Ow, cramp, cramp, cramp. Cramp can stop me."

As Ted rubbed his sore calf, he saw the monkey standing nearby with the hat in his hand. The monkey laughed.

"Okay, I have an idea," said Ted, removing an item from his pack. He held it out. "We'll trade. Sandwich for hat."

Ted reached for the hat. The monkey reached for the sandwich.

Now the monkey had a grip on Ted's hat *and* sandwich. Ted tried to pull the hat out of the monkey's hands. The monkey pulled back. What fun! Ted and the monkey rocked back and forth in a game of tug of war.

Frustrated as he was, Ted couldn't help laughing. "Okay. We're not really making any progress here."

Ted stopped rocking and the monkey stopped rocking too.

In the lull, Ted pulled and *thwop!* — he slapped his prize on top of his head.

"Ah haaa!" he cried triumphantly.

Then Ted noticed that the monkey was smiling and wearing his hat. That must mean the sandwich was on his own head. Ugh! He groaned as he felt the mustard oozing down onto his nose.

The monkey smiled and held out Ted's hat. Another wonderful game! Ted took the hat and handed the monkey the sandwich. The monkey slapped the sandwich on his own head — happy as any monkey could be.

Once Ted, Edu, and the porters were back on their trail through the jungle, Ted returned to Bloomsberry's map and counted his steps carefully.

"One hundred ninety-two, one hundred ninety-three, one hundred ninety-four." Suddenly Ted found the path blocked by the little monkey, smiling sweetly up at him. Ted stepped around the monkey, trying not to lose count. "Not now, monkey . . . one hundred ninety-five, one hundred ninety-six, one hundred ninety-seven." The monkey moved in front of Ted again. Ted stepped over him. "One ninety-monkey, one hundred ninety-nine, two hundred! Okay! The map says to look for two mufuti bushes and we will find 'X.' "

The porters parted the bushes and Ted raised the binoculars to his eyes. "Okay, I know it's here! I can feel it!" he cried. He scanned the horizon.

The monkey jumped up and down on a branch, holding his hands over his eyes like binoculars.

"Ah! There it is!" A huge monkey shrine filled Ted's field of view. The idol was as magnificent as Mr. Bloomsberry had described it: a solemn monkey face with a sturdy, imposing body. It was sitting in a stone cave decorated with pretty geometric shapes — a half circle with smaller circles around it.

"It's awesome. It's spectacular. It's" — suddenly the idol disappeared — "gone?"

Ted lowered his binoculars and looked into the bush. There, smack in front of him, was the "Lost Shrine of Zagawa"— all three inches of it! The stone monkey idol had tipped over onto its side.

"This can't be it," cried Ted. "It's supposed to be huge. *That* isn't huge. That's the opposite of huge. I need the *giant* monkey." Edu held up the journal and Ted compared the little statue to Bloomsberry's sketch. The two were exactly the same — except for the fact that Ted's was only a fraction of the size of Bloomsberry's.

Ted peered at the inscription on the wall of the little alcove.

"Wait, this looks like ancient Swatabi." He tried translating it: "'Turn your eye to the light, go from blindness to sight.'"

Ted thought for a moment. "Hold on. That's a clue!" he cried. "'Turn your eye to the light.'" He looked up into the sky. "All right, now I'm looking directly into the sun. It's very bright . . . it's starting to sting, I'm not going to lie to you. . . . Okay, now it's burning!"

Ted covered his eyes with his hands and screamed in pain. "AAAARGH! I singed my corneas! I'M BLIND! Oh, I'm blind!"

Edu handed Ted his canteen and he doused his eyes with water.

The little monkey giggled and clapped his hands. How funny the man with the yellow hat was!

"Time to pack up," cried Edu to his porters.

The curious monkey stayed and watched the man muttering to his little statue.

"I traveled ten thousand miles for a paperweight." Ted sighed. "What am I going to tell Mr. Bloomsberry?"

At the worst possible moment, Ted's cell phone rang. He was amazed that he even got reception so far out in the jungle. He looked at the caller ID, which said "Bloomsberry." He gulped.

"Hello?"

"Ted, it's me. Have you found it yet?" asked Mr. Bloomsberry.

"Yeah. I'm looking at it right now."

"How does it look?"

"Well, there is a size issue, sir. I'll send you a photo so you can see for yourself." Ted centered the statue in the viewfinder of his cell-phone camera and pushed send.

Back in the big city, Mr. Bloomsberry and Bloomsberry junior saw what looked like a gigantic monkey idol filling their computer screen.

"Do you see it, sir?" asked Ted nervously.

"I do," said Mr. Bloomsberry, his voice choked with emotion.

"Sir . . . are you crying?" asked Ted.

"Oh, Ted . . ." Mr. Bloomsberry sniffled.

"I-I'll explain it all when I get back," said Ted.

"No need to explain, Ted. Got to go," replied Mr. Bloomsberry.

Before he could say anything else, Ted heard the click of a handset being replaced. He couldn't believe he hadn't been able to tell his boss and good friend the truth.

In his office Mr. Bloomsberry wiped the tears from his eyes. "I can't believe it. It's even bigger than I imagined!"

"Hurray, we're saved," said his son Junior without enthusiasm.

Mr. Bloomsberry looked ready to celebrate. But back in the jungle, Ted sat despondently, staring at the measly statue in his hands.

"Time to go, Mr. Ted!" called Edu.

Ted sighed.

The monkey felt sorry for his funny friend in the yellow hat who suddenly looked so sad. How could he cheer him up? The monkey had an idea. He swooped down from his branch and swiped the hat.

"Let me guess," said Ted, looking up. The monkey waved the hat at him, inviting him to play.

Ted gave the monkey a sad smile. "You know what? Keep the hat."

He turned and followed the porters. The monkey trotted behind him, confused. Ted turned and looked at him.

"No, really, it's yours."

Nobody had ever given the monkey a gift before. He turned it around in his hands and inspected it happily.

"Don't worry, it's the new khaki," said Ted.

The monkey watched as the man and his party rode away in a jeep. It looked like time for some fast action!

Heading Home Empty-Handed

When they reached the harbor, Ted drove the jeep across the crowded dock and pulled up next to the ship. He got out and shuffled glumly up the gangway.

The little monkey swung high over the harbor town, one hand hanging on to a vine, the other still holding on to the yellow hat. He spotted Ted boarding the ship. He had to catch up. He swung faster.

Plop! He jumped down into a stack of bowls on top of a woman's head. As she approached the dock, the monkey sprang out of the top bowl and landed on a shipping drum. One, two, three — he sprang from drum to drum. Then he was off — *squawk!* — into a flock of chickens, sending them scattering in all directions.

Ted didn't notice the commotion. He gazed into the distance, unable to think of anything but his own failure, and wondering what he would say to Mr. Bloomsberry.

"Mr. Ted!" called Edu from the dock. "Your trunk!"

Ted looked down.

"I throw to you. You catch!" cried Edu. He flung Ted's suitcase up.

"Uh-oh," said Ted as he watched it hit the side of the ship. His books and clothes tumbled out of the suitcase and dropped into the water below.

"Bye-bye, nonyellow things," Ted said sadly.

The little monkey scurried through a maze of legs on the dock and climbed up onto a stack of crates. He saw the longshoremen untying the ship. They were pushing off! The monkey had to hurry. If only he could fly like the seagulls. Without thinking, he leapt toward the ship. Out he went over the water . . . then back down . . . *splash!*

Luckily the monkey caught hold of a big chain and soon found himself riding the rising anchor like an elevator up to the ship. He slipped through the anchor-chain hole and jumped down into the hold of the ship. Above him on deck, he heard the man's familiar voice.

"Mr. Bloomsberry, uh, I would just like to say in my defense, that . . ." Ted was muttering to himself, rehearsing his explanation. "Sir, when we set out on certain adventures in life —"

The monkey peered through the hatch. There was the man in yellow! He climbed up onto a stack of crates. But just as he reached the hatch, one of the sailors slid it shut. *Thump.* Too late! The little monkey stood in the dark, confused.

"— sometimes, well, sometimes they don't quite go as planned . . ." Ted's rehearsal continued.

The monkey squeezed back out the anchor hole and peered into one of the ship's portholes. He tapped on the glass, trying to get the man's attention.

But Ted just went on staring at his feet and muttering. "Of course, I'm really sorry. I'm *extra* sorry. . . ."

The monkey scampered back down to the cargo hold. At least the man was close by. He had come to the right place.

The little monkey stopped to survey the cavernous cargo hold. As he investigated the labyrinth of crates and steamer trunks, possibilities formed in his mind. A shiny brass latch glinted enticingly from one of the trunks. He just had to touch it. POP! The latch sprang open and an avalanche of clothes came cascading down around him. He jumped out of the pile like a jack-in-the-box, wearing a pair of britches on his head. What fun!

The monkey looked for other latches and buttons to push. Soon there were more colorful explosions of clothes.

BRRRRROOOM! Oops, what was that? The monkey had accidentally pushed the ignition of the big forklift. It zoomed out of control and crashed into a stack of crates. As the forklift stalled to a stop, fresh fruit came tumbling out of the broken crates.

Yum! thought the little monkey, and dove right in.

Meanwhile Ted had squeezed into his tiny cabin and was trying to get settled for the night. "So glad I upgraded," he said to himself sarcastically. The ship rolled forward and Ted whacked his knee on the dresser. The ship rolled the other way and a drawer slid out and conked him in the head.

When Ted tried to open a small package of peanuts for his supper, he almost couldn't do it in the small space. Using all his strength, he finally managed to tear the packaging, but all the nuts went flying. They trickled down a grate in the floor.

"Awww — not the honey-roasted goodness," Ted lamented. What else could go wrong today? Sighing, Ted fell back onto his bed, hitting his head. Hard.

In contrast, the monkey down in the cargo hold lay on top of a pallet of fruit. His belly was distended, he was so full. Curling up with Ted's hat, he went right to sleep.

Monkey in the Big City

A few days later, as the ship was docking in the city harbor, one of the sailors opened the hatch. A well-fed monkey leapt onto the deck. The deck hand exclaimed, "Hey, a monkey with a hat!" But the monkey didn't stop. He was on a mission.

He climbed up to the ship's gunnel and took in his first view of the big city: skyscrapers taller than jungle trees, elevated trains rumbling past like parades of elephants, airplanes zooming overhead like giant silver flamingos! It was all a little scary, but the monkey was determined to find his new friend.

"Where ya goin', yellow?" a deep voice called out from somewhere below on the dock. The monkey spotted Ted.

"The Bloomsberry Museum," Ted said as he climbed into the man's taxi. "And you know, I'll give you ten bucks extra if you'll stop calling me yellow."

"You got it, sunshine," quipped the cabbie.

The little monkey watched as the yellow cab zoomed off. He bounded ashore. He immediately spotted a yellow car and ran across the street. He jumped onto the cab's trunk and tapped on the rear window. But it was not Ted inside. A woman in red had turned around and was screaming.

The startled monkey quickly leapt onto the roof of the cab. He looked around for Ted's vehicle, but yellow cabs were everywhere!

As Ted's cab, several cars ahead, stopped at a red light, Ted watched a city bus pull up beside them. Plastered across the side was an advertisement for the museum: "THE LOST SHRINE OF ZAGAWA — ZAGAWA 4O FEET TALL!"

"Huh?" Ted could not believe his eyes. Unfortunately, that was not all. Ted was horrified to discover that all over the city, Mr. Bloomsberry had billboards ordered announcing the new exhibit.

"That's not right," cried Ted as the cab passed yet another sign. "The shrine is not forty feet tall!"

"I heard it was fifty feet tall," said his cabbie. "That bad boy is a monster! I can't wait to see it. I'm taking the whole family."

"Uh, yeah, well . . . I hope you get seats up front," Ted said meaningfully.

While Ted sat glumly contemplating the little statuette in his hand, the monkey was wreaking havoc with the traffic, jumping from cab top to cab top, frightening their occupants.

But what a great ride he was having! The monkey leapt to another cab. "Yeah, sure, I've seen everything in this town," said the cabbie to the two tourists in the back seat. The monkey poked his head in the driver-side window. "Oh, yeah, a monkey. Seen it," bragged the cabbie while the tourists hurried to snap a photo.

The camera's bright flash made the monkey blink. What was that? As the confused little monkey rubbed his eyes, a gust of wind blew his yellow hat away.

He continued leaping from car to car, chasing it down the street. The wind blew it to the ground. The monkey jumped down into the busy street. A monstrous truck was coming right toward him. Instinctively he ducked under his hat and felt the whoosh of the truck's engine as it passed over him.

This development was too scary, even for a curious monkey. Seeking a safe spot, he jumped on the back of another truck and nestled into a big spool of cable. He hugged his yellow hat to his chest. Where, oh, where, was the man?

Ted was nearby, stuck in a traffic jam.

"Must be construction," said Ted's cabbie.

Ted looked at the sea of gridlocked cars. "Uh, sir, I'll just get out here. This'll work. I'm just going to go home, call Mr. Bloomsberry, and explain everything."

"Sure. Whatever," agreed the cabbie. "Twelve fifty, pal."

From his perch in the cable spool, the little monkey noticed a familiar beacon of yellow. There was his friend! But where was he going? The monkey had to find out. He swung away from his nest and hopped from car to car, and then from rooftop to rooftop, in hot pursuit. Finally he saw Ted headed toward the door of one of the tall buildings. That must be the man's home!

No Pets Allowed

Ted stepped into the marble lobby of his apartment building and greeted Ivan, the doorman. With his Slavic features and thick mustache, he was a very imposing figure. Ivan sniffed the air and glared at Ted suspiciously.

As he went to the elevator Ted felt the doorman looming over him like a musclebound shot-putter. "Good talking to you . . . take care," Ted said as he quickly escaped into the elevator.

Outside, the little monkey watched a glass box rising up the side of the building. The man was inside! The monkey grabbed his hat and scrambled up the fire escape. Up, up, up he went until he saw the box stop and the man vanish back into the building. The monkey crept from windowsill to windowsill, peeking into each one.

Inside his apartment Ted tossed his keys onto the table and

slumped on the couch. “Home,” he sighed. “Okay, I just need two seconds of quiet.”

Two seconds later the phone rang. “All right, I didn't mean that literally,” Ted said, lifting his head from the couch to check the phone's view screen. The caller ID said “Bloomsberry.” Ted groaned. “How does he do that?”

“Hello?” he said, picking up the receiver.

“Ted!” cried Bloomsberry.

“Hi, Mr. Bloomsberry. I just walked in the door —”

“Get down here!” shouted Mr. Bloomsberry over the noise of a big crowd. “I've arranged a press conference! You're the hero of the moment!”

Ted heard people cheering in the background.

“You hear that, son? It's all for you!” cried Mr. Bloomsberry. “Have you seen the surprise?”

“Surprise, sir?” queried Ted.

“Look out your front window. . . .”

“My window?” Ted parted the curtains. There, on the building across the street, was a huge billboard advertising the lost shrine. Ted couldn't bear to look!

The monkey saw the curtains open and tried to get the man's

attention. But the drapes closed again with a swoosh.

"Ah, speechless," said Mr. Bloomsberry. "I knew you'd like it. In all my years I have never been —"

"Uh, Mr. Bloomsberry, I have to tell you something."

"Yes?"

As Ted struggled to figure out how to tell Mr. Bloomsberry the awful truth, the monkey found an open window and slipped inside. He fell to the floor with a thud. And the big hat plopped down over him.

Ted glanced in the direction of the sound. He did a double take. Was that *his* yellow hat sitting on the floor?

"My hat!" he cried.

"Sure, wear your hat!" replied Mr. Bloomsberry. "Wear your best suit — just get down here!"

Ted hung up and looked around the room as if a practical joker might be hiding somewhere. "My yellow hat from Africa? No, no. This can't be the same hat. . . ."

The little monkey peeked out from under the brim.

"It *is* the same hat! And the same monkey!" Ted stared at the monkey in disbelief. "Wait! You followed me all the way from Africa" — the monkey ducked back under the hat — "to play peekaboo?"

The monkey peeked again.

"No, no. I don't want to play peekaboo."

Suddenly Ted heard a loud knock at his door.

"Seventeen-B, open up!"

It was Ivan!

Ted picked up the hat, but the monkey was gone.

Ivan continued pounding on the door. "Open up!" he shouted.

Ted answered his door. "Oh, hi, Ivan," he said, acting surprised to see him.

Ivan poked his nose in the door and sniffed. "I'm smelling pet," he declared in his heavy accent.

"Pet? No. No pet here," Ted dithered. "Can't have a pet. Isn't there a no-pet policy?"

"Yes." Ivan pushed past him and stalked around the room.

"Hey, you can't just barge in here!" cried Ted.

Ivan got down on his hands and knees and began sniffing around the place like a bloodhound.

"Okay, apparently you can."

As Ivan approached the lounge chair in the living room, the monkey popped up over its back and peered down at him. Ivan sniffed up the back of the chair. The monkey ducked down.

"Aha!" cried Ivan.

"What?" asked Ted.

"Just practicing for when I find pet," growled Ivan.

The monkey scampered across the floor, climbed up on the dining room table, grabbed the chandelier, and started swinging.

Ted gasped. "No. Down. Down. Down. No. No. No!"

Ivan turned and glared at him. "Why you yell when I'm right next to you?"

"Uh . . . no reason."

The monkey raced into the kitchen and Ted watched him nervously.

Following Ted's glance, Ivan ran to the fridge, yanked it open, and sniffed.

"Aha!" he cried.

"What?"

"Milk is sour, don't drink."

As Ivan closed the refrigerator door, Ted saw the monkey in plain sight on the countertop. Thinking quickly, Ted picked up a dish and hurled it at the wall in the next room.

"Bingo!" cried Ivan, following the noise.

Ted scooped up the monkey in his hat. "New game. New game," he whispered urgently. "Hide and seek." He carried the monkey around the corner to the bathroom. "Okay, stay right there," he told him. "Good monkey."

Ted put his hat on and left the bathroom, closing the door behind him.

The monkey rattled the toilet paper on its roller. It unrolled. He was fascinated. Soon the whole thing had been unraveled. The monkey looked around and saw more rolls on a high shelf!

"Did you hear something?" asked Ivan.

"No," said Ted, blocking the way to the bathroom.

Clang! Clang!

"How about that?" asked Ivan.

"Nope."

The toilet flushed.

"If you're asking, I didn't hear that either," said Ted.

"Move self, please." Ivan pushed the door open. "Aha!" he cried triumphantly. Fluffy ribbons of toilet paper covered everything.

"I unroll it ahead of time," explained Ted. "Helps when you're in a rush."

Ted looked at the wall above the toilet. The air-vent door was hanging open!

Ivan began to search through the mounds of toilet paper.

"Where the pet? Where the pet? Can't find the pet nowhere. Very strange. Nose does not lie."

"Well, that was fun," crooned Ted. "Next time we'll have to do it at your place, okay, Ivan?"

"If I find pet, you are evicted!" threatened Ivan as he stormed out the front door.

Breathless, Ted rushed back to investigate the air shaft. "Monkey? Oh, Mr. Monkey?" he called out. He heard clanging noises above him, in the walls. "Oh, no, that's trouble."

Paint in the Penthouse

As the monkey explored the air ducts, some interesting music caught his ear. It was so beautiful — different from anything he'd ever heard. He wanted to see where it was coming from. Using all four paws, he shimmied up the narrow, silvery air shaft toward the music. A glint of light shone through a small vent. The monkey peered through the slatted grate at the posh penthouse apartment of Ms. Plushbottom.

The eager monkey popped open the vent and hopped into the dining room.

The monkey trapezed from the chandelier to a chair and then a table, tracking the music to a speaker on the floor. The music played softly for a moment. The monkey put his ear up against the speaker's fabric covering. Was the pretty music in there? Suddenly the music blasted forth again. The monkey stumbled away from the speaker. *Sploosh!* His foot landed in something wet and slippery.

Ms. Plushbottom had been about to have her apartment painted, and the monkey had landed in a tray of green paint. He made a perfect footprint on the rug. Wonderful! Pails full of different colors stood in a row near one wall. Ms. Plushbottom wasn't happy with any of them. She was going to send them back to the decorator's shop tomorrow. But the monkey thought they were great. He had an idea! He began to fill the wall with handprints in every color.

In the bathroom Ms. Plushbottom was relaxing in a large tub filled with bubbles. She had placed soothing cucumber slices over her closed eyes. Just like an aspiring diva, she sang along with the opera music at top volume. "Positively divine," she commented.

The monkey was painting away when he saw some bubbles drifting out of the bathroom. He poked one with his paint-covered fingertip. POP! Wow. Curious, he tasted the next bubble to float by and grimaced. Yuck! They were not for eating.

He decided to follow the bubble trail to Ms. Plushbottom's bathroom. He approached the tub and dipped his finger in the foamy water. A lovely rainbow of colors spread out over the bubbles. Delighted, the monkey stuck his painted hands in too.

Meanwhile Ted bounded out the window and up the fire escape to catch the naughty monkey. He gripped the rickety metal ladder, trying to forget his fear of heights.

"Don't look down. Don't look," he cautioned himself. "Rickety's okay, just as long as there's no wind."

Whoosh! Thwop! A big gust of wind blew a newspaper page against his face. Then his foot slipped. "Oh, sweet mother of science!" he cried, dangling by one hand from a rung. The sights were dizzying from this height.

"Oh, no — cramp, cramp," he added as he hoisted himself back up onto the ladder.

Finally he reached the top of the fire escape and flung himself gratefully onto the penthouse ledge. He paused for a moment to catch his breath. He shooed away a flock of pigeons that had landed on the rim of his hat. "Okay, fellas, last stop. Everybody off."

As the birds flew away, Ted found a skylight and peered down into — DISASTER!

"Oh, no!" he cried. Who would leave so many open cans of paint lying around?

Ted leaned his forehead against the skylight in despair and it swung open unexpectedly. "Aaaaaaah!" He lost his balance and d down into Ms. Plushbottom's living room. He was lucky to land in her comfy chair. Right away he noted a suspicious trail of brightly colored footprints leading out of the room. He followed them to the bathroom door. He peeked in.

"Oh, such a beautiful song!" exclaimed Ms. Plushbottom, still oblivious to the little monkey who was now pouring pails of paint into her tub.

"Oh, boy." Ted waved his hat to get the monkey's attention. "Monkey, peekaboo. Peekaboo, monkey," he whispered desperately.

The monkey was delighted to see him again. He jumped up and down and giggled.

"Shhhh," warned Ted. "Shhh. Monkey, no!"

But it was too late. Ms. Plushbottom had heard them. She peeled the cucumbers off her eyes and — "Aah! What's that?" she gasped.

"Do yourself a favor, you're gonna wanna put those cucumbers back on," said Ted, grabbing the monkey and running.

Ms. Plushbottom rose indignantly from her bath. "Ooo — ooo — oooh!" she screamed, her voice rising to a high C when she saw herself in the full-length mirror, covered from head to toe in multicolored bubbles. She hit the intercom button.

"Ivannnnnnnn!"

But Ivan must have kept looking for the illicit pet because just as Ted reached the front door, the doorman burst in.

"I knew it!" he cried as he saw Ted with the monkey.

Ted backed away.

"You are red-handed with pet!"

Ted set the monkey down. "And while we're on the subject, I think you have a serious pest problem in this building, Ivan. I mean, don't you spray for jungle animals every spring?"

The monkey reached up and grasped Ted's hand affectionately. "Let go, you're not helping," whispered Ted.

At that moment a rainbow-swirled Ms. Plushbottom stormed into the room. "Look at my walls!"

"And you . . ." Ted paused accusingly.

"Moi?" asked Ms. Plushbottom.

"You hired a monkey to paint your apartment? How do you sleep at night?"

But it was no use trying to distract them. Ivan pointed to the wall, where the monkey had painted a self-portrait with his friend in the yellow suit holding him.

"He is your monkey!" cried Ivan. "Now what do you say?"

"Come on, that could be any guy in a yellow suit," tried Ted. "Double-breasted, forty-six-long . . ."

"Ivaaaan!" Miss Plushbottom screamed impatiently.

Ivan lunged for them.

"Well, that was fun. Bye-bye!" Ted scooped up his monkey and raced to the window.

"You can't leave. I have to throw you out!" shouted Ivan.

Ted and the monkey climbed down the rickety fire escape.

Ivan stuck his head out the window and shouted at them, "Hey, you are no more Seventeen B. You are kicked from building."

"Just to be clear — the monkey's kicked, not me, right?" asked Ted.

"GET OUT!" roared Ivan.

Ted started climbing down. He was almost down when in his rush he slipped and fell. His foot caught between two rungs. "Oh, oh, oh," he gasped. "Ow, ow, ow!"

He was dangling upside down over the sidewalk!

The monkey jumped off his back and landed easily.

"What am I going to do with you?" Ted sighed.

Museum Mayhem

As Ted dropped to the sidewalk, he saw a sign. A pet-shop sign! This could be the answer to his problem. He entered, carefully concealing the monkey behind his back.

A bored sales clerk lounged behind the counter, playing his Game Boy.

"Hello, my good sir," Ted greeted him. "How are you today?"

The clerk did not look up.

"You know what? Don't answer me. Because today is your lucky day," continued Ted. "Today you have been given a free monkey! Yes, you heard me right — a free monkey!"

Ted produced the sweet, beaming animal.

Still engrossed in his game, the clerk gave his stock response: "Thank you for your donation of a dog, cat, bird, other —"

Ding. The bell over the door rang.

"Huh?" The clerk looked up over his shoulder into the smiling face of a little monkey. Ted had already slipped out the door.

The monkey pushed one of the buttons on the clerk's handheld game.

"Hey!" the clerk scolded. Then he saw the results. "Hey. Level six! Sweet."

Outside on the street, Ted gave a sigh of relief. "Well played, Ted," he said to himself. "He belongs with animals. In no time he'll have them all playing peekaboo and monkey-in-the-middle. He's a natural."

Ted waded out into the sea of pedestrians.

A pretty woman seemed to be staring right at him, smiling. "Hi, cutie," she said.

Ted smiled back proudly. "Thank you kindly."

He was beginning to think that perhaps he had underestimated the appeal of his yellow suit, when he saw a little ball of brown fur by his side. "Aaaaaaah!"

The monkey reached up and took Ted's hand.

"What? Wait, how . . . ? But I left you back at the pet store," cried Ted, forgetting that the clever little monkey had already managed to follow him all the way from Africa.

"Okay, come on," he sighed. "I'll figure out what to do with you after I talk to Mr. Bloomsberry."

The monkey watched, fascinated, as two little kids tugged playfully on their father's arms and pant legs. The monkey did the same to Ted.

The monkey saw a baby sucking her thumb. The monkey jumped into Ted's arms and tried sucking his thumb too.

"Yuck," Ted said as the monkey scrambled up on his shoulders and started picking through his hair. The monkey had seen a little boy riding high on his father's shoulders.

"Ooh, that tickles." Ted chuckled.

A couple of girls stopped and stared at him.

"He's grooming me," explained Ted. "Everyone's doing it. They're getting small monkeys and . . . never mind."

Down the street, Ted could see the news trucks pulling up outside the Oswald J. Bloomsberry Museum. He scooped up the monkey, snuck around to the back, and tried to reach his arm in and unlatch a half-open window. The monkey easily slipped through the narrow opening and unlatched the window from the inside.

"Showoff," said Ted.

They tiptoed down the dim, echoing hallway toward Ted's

office. But Ted stopped dead in his tracks when he saw the new gift-shop display. Gone were the glow-in-the-dark star stickers. Everything was Zagawa! Racks of "I'M GAGA FOR ZAGAWA" T-shirts, key chains, and bobble-head dolls loomed like monsters in a bad dream.

"Oh, no. What have they done?" he moaned.

Enthralled, the monkey picked up a shiny Zagawa snow globe and shook it.

"These are inaccurate. There's no snow in that part of Africa," whined Ted. But African snow globes were the least of his problems. Already he could hear the throng of excited reporters entering at the other end of the hallway. And Mr. Bloomsberry was telling them Ted would answer all their questions soon!

"Run, monkey. Run!" he cried. The two of them raced down the hall and ducked into Ted's office.

Ted closed his door and slumped in his chair. "What am I going to do?"

Thwap, thwap. Thwap, thwap. Thwap, thwap. The monkey played with the venetian blinds, opening and closing them over and over.

"Hey. Monkey. Quiet!" yelled Ted.

George, curious as always, leans in for a closer look.

Fun in the jungle

George makes a
special new friend.

This stowaway monkey makes a lucky find.

George has never seen a city before. It's amazing!

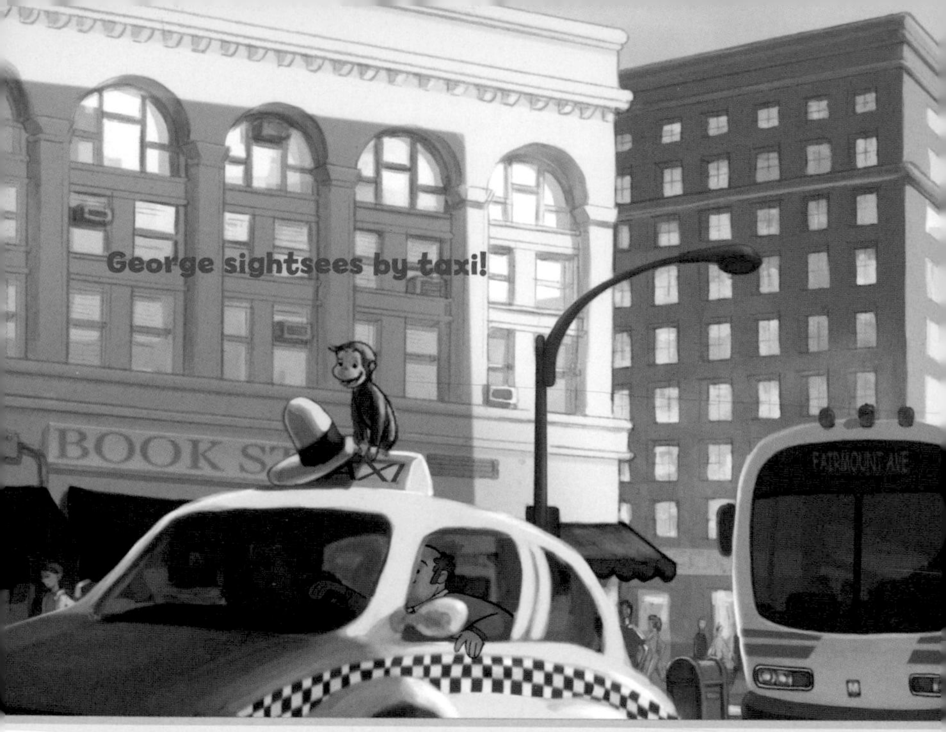

George sightsees by taxi!

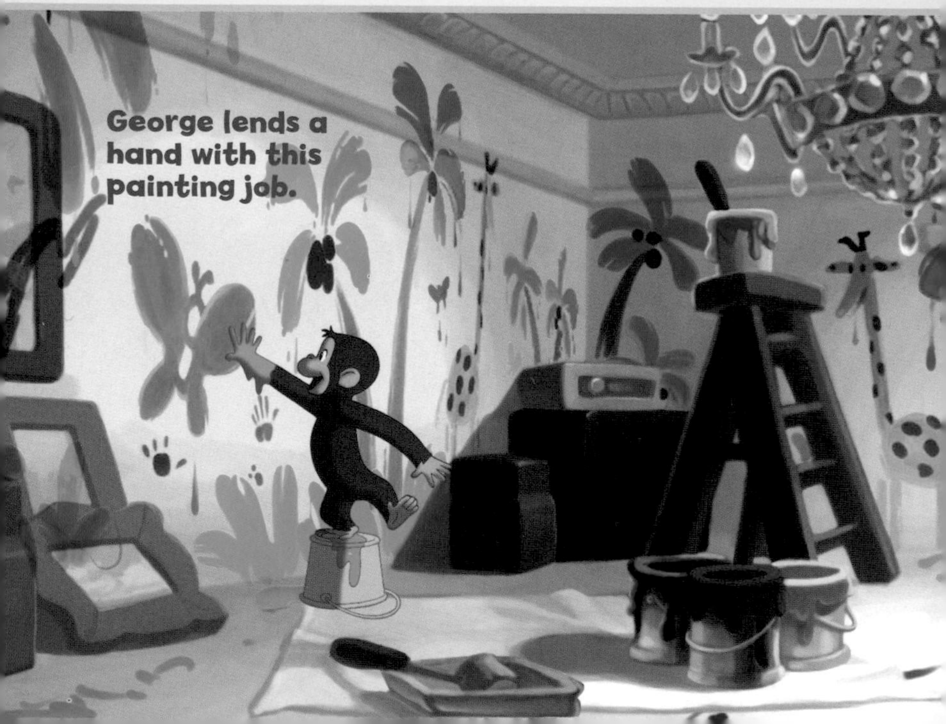

George lends a hand with this painting job.

George has the best of intentions when he visits the museum . . .

. . . and when he grabs a bunch of balloons.

Ted and George
have fast become
the best of friends

Together they
find the lost
Shrine of Zagawa.

Ted and George zoom off on their next great adventure!

Over in his own office, Junior was packing up his parking-lot model. "Well, we gave it a shot, didn't we?" he said to the model. "I mean, monkey statues, they come and go, but parking lots are forever."

Hearing the commotion coming from Ted's office, Junior looked up and spotted the infamous yellow hat in the window. "Well, look who's back," he said. The blinds went on flipping open, closed, open, closed. He saw Ted in his yellow suit. "What is he — officially the golden child now?"

Junior leaned out his window and he could hear Ted muttering to himself: "I've got problems. Oh, do I have problems."

Junior brightened. "Glorious day. Ted has problems."

"I have to tell Mr. Bloomsberry the truth. The horrible —"

"Horrible?" wondered Junior aloud. He climbed out onto the ledge and inched closer to the window, the better to eavesdrop on Ted's mutterings.

" — awful — " said Ted.

"Awful?"

" — devastatingly crushing truth."

Junior grinned with glee. "Devastatingly crushing?"

"His enormous idol looks like it came out of a cereal box."

"Huh. That must be some huge box of cereal, or else . . ."

Junior felt hope rising for the first time in days.

"It's only three inches tall," moaned Ted.

Junior did a little happy dance on the ledge. "Yes! This is great. What a great day for parking lots."

Whoops. He slipped off the ledge and fell into the bushes below.

"Ow."

In Ted's office the monkey was spinning a globe, making a clackety racket, when Ted heard someone knocking. He tried to get the monkey to shush.

Before Ted could get to the door, it swung open and he was greeted by Clovis, the museum's resident inventor.

"Ted! Are you serious?" asked Clovis.

Ted glanced over his shoulder at the spinning globe, but the monkey was nowhere in sight.

"Clovis, I can explain —" started Ted.

"I should hope so," said Clovis, "because that is a lot of yellow for one man."

Ted stopped. "I thought you were colorblind."

"*That* I can see!"

Ted quickly ushered Clovis out the door before he needed to explain anything more than a yellow suit. He glanced nervously over his shoulder as they exited, and there was the monkey slowly spinning on his ceiling fan! He locked the door behind him.

"Here's a bill for my services," said Clovis.

"Two thousand dollars? What's this for?" asked Ted.

Clovis led him to the Lost Shrine of Zagawa exhibit. A huge empty alcove decorated with native African flora and fauna awaited the Zagawa idol. Mr. Bloomsberry was there to greet Ted.

"It's the exhibition stage for the lost shrine," explained Mr. Bloomsberry.

"Mr. Bloomsberry!" exclaimed Ted. "I need to tell you some—"

"Watch this!" Bloomsberry interrupted. He pushed a button on a remote-control device and a loud recorded voice boomed: "Behold the eighth wonder of the world."

"Clovis whipped it up. Doesn't it take your breath away?" he asked.

"It does," Ted gulped.

In Ted's office, the little monkey explored. He found a fish tank with a small model of the museum inside. The monkey was fascinated to see a miniature dinosaur skeleton head pop in and out of the museum's dome. It growled every time it popped up and the monkey had fun making growling noises back.

"Okay, let's get down to business. Where's the shrine?" asked Bloomsberry, back at the exhibit space.

Ted pulled the small idol out of his pocket and carefully set it down in the cavernous alcove.

"What's that?" asked Bloomsberry.

Ted pressed the button on the remote. "Behold the eighth wonder of the world."

"But, Ted . . . that can't be the idol. I don't understand — we saw the picture. The statue is huge."

"I'm sorry, sir. But that's it. I've been trying to tell you"— Ted held up his digital photo next to the little idol — "this is *this*."

"What are we going to do?" cried Mr. Bloomsberry.

There was no time to think, because at that very moment an exultant Bloomsberry junior was escorting the crowd of eager reporters into the exhibit room. "Here he is. Right this way. No pushing, we'll all get a shot."

Junior leaned over and whispered to Ted, "Sorry I couldn't hold them any longer. They can't wait for you to tell them about the massively huge, gigantic, enormous idol, Ted."

Junior checked the news cameras to make sure they were rolling. He couldn't wait to see Ted's embarrassing admission recorded on film for all eternity.

Ted reluctantly approached the microphone. "Ahhh. Any questions?" he asked timidly.

Dozens of reporters jostled each other in their excitement. "Excuse me! Was it difficult finding a boat big enough to bring it back?" asked one.

"No, no. Didn't have a problem on the boat thing," answered Ted. "Yeah, it fit nicely."

Back in Ted's office, the little monkey blew bubbles in the fish tank. The fish inside rode the air currents and jumped out of the bowl, loving the fun. Suddenly the monkey perked up and listened to the amplified noise. He recognized that voice! It was the man in yellow. He climbed up and squeezed out the transom window over Ted's door and headed toward the exhibit.

"Over here!" called another reporter. "When you first saw the idol, did the sheer size of it frighten you?"

"Uh, yes," replied Ted. "Very much so."

"Where's the idol now?" "Yeah, let's see it!" cried the reporters.

Bloomsberry climbed onstage behind Ted and put a reassuring hand on his shoulder.

"It's, uh, close. It's very close," stammered Ted.

"What do you say to the experts who predict that this idol will rival King Tut? Is it made of solid granite?"

"Uhhh, yes, yes. Any other . . ."

Behind the reporters in the nearby atrium Ted noticed the little monkey hopping from one display to the next, swinging on the artificial trees.

"Can you tell how old it is?" "When can we see it?" "How much does it weigh?" "Does it have magical powers?" The reporters' questions became a blur to Ted, who stood transfixed as the monkey climbed up the leg of an immense brontosaur skeleton.

"Did you make friends with the local people?" "Are you going to write a book?" "Do you have a movie deal?" The reporters' questions kept coming.

The monkey tightrope-walked along the dinosaur's backbone.

"Oh, no, that's not a good idea," murmured Ted.

The reporters began to look puzzled. "It's not? Why?"

"No!" shouted Ted. "No, no, no. You're a bad monkey!"

"What'd you just call me?" asked one of the reporters.

Mr. Bloomsberry covered for Ted. "This is very common when you come back from the jungle. The sun is very hot there."

The reporters exchanged glances.

By now the monkey had walked way out on the dinosaur's long neck and was perched on its head.

"Hey, excuse me," interrupted Junior. "Can we please get back to questions regarding when we will actually see the idol? Ted, you were saying . . ."

The dinosaur's neck made a loud snapping sound.

"Oh, no . . ." muttered Ted. He pushed through the crowd, his eyes riveted on the monkey.

"Hey, where's he going?" cried Junior.

Crrreeeaaakkkkk. . . . The dinosaur's neck began to tip downward. *Crack!*

"Noooooo, not the *Apatosaurus* — formerly known as the *Brontosaurus* . . . !" cried Ted.

The press followed him as he rushed to the skeleton.

"Hey! Monkey!" he shouted. He tried to stabilize the dinosaur's forelegs. But it was too late! The bones began to heave and crack with the stress.

The monkey crawled into the dinosaur's skull and rode the skeleton like a crazy astronaut piloting an enormous ship. All the cameras were on them as the big bones fell and Ted emerged from the pile of rubble on the floor.

"Wow, I didn't see that coming," said Junior.

"Oh, Ted," moaned Mr. Bloomsberry. "We're doomed."

Soon after that Junior escorted Ted to the door, with the little monkey trotting happily behind them. "Sorry, Ted," said Junior. "There is no need to come back — unless of course you're carrying a forty-foot version of your little trinket."

Homeless

Furious, Ted stormed to the nearest phone booth, flipped through the yellow pages, and found the listing for animal control. He punched in the number.

The operator answered: "Hello, animal control. How can I help you?"

"Could you send someone over to the Bloomsberry Museum right away?" asked Ted. "We have a very dangerous monkey."

The little monkey pressed his lips against the glass side of the phone booth — Ted had left him outside — and puffed out his cheeks.

"Uh-huh. Describe dangerous, sir," she requested.

"He's frothing at the mouth, he's got teeth like Ginsu knives and . . . and . . . crazy eyes! He's a killer! Listen to this!"

Ted held the phone at arm's length and hooted and bellowed

like a vicious ape. "Put that child down! Oh, the horror! *I can't watch!*" he screamed.

The little monkey laughed, entertained.

"Sir, we just closed," said the animal control operator. "But I can leave a message."

"What am I supposed to do with this monkey?" asked Ted.

"I'm sure I don't know," she replied. "Thank you for calling the animal-control hotline."

Ted heard a dial tone. "Hello?"

The little monkey was hanging upside down from the top of the phone booth, peering in through the glass.

"You. Down," ordered Ted.

The monkey climbed down. He looked up at Ted with sleepy eyes. He stretched out his arms and yawned.

"Okay. Listen. I'm only watching you till . . ." Ted yawned too. "Don't do that," he chided the monkey. He glanced at his watch and sighed. "Maybe you're right. It's been a long day. I have an idea."

A little later, Ted stretched out on a park bench, trying to get comfortable. "Oh, this is great. . . . This is a great idea. . . . I'm so comfortable," he muttered sarcastically.

The little monkey cocked his head and listened as Ted

continued muttering. He looked up at the dark clouds beginning to cover the moon. He moved off toward a nearby tree.

Thunder rumbled and rain began to pour down on Ted's head. He sighed, helpless, wide-awake, and exhausted.

The monkey climbed up the tree and began shaking the branches with all his might.

"Hey, shake all you want, monkey," said Ted. "There's no bananas in there. But if you find a forty-foot idol, let me know."

He picked a wind-blown poster off the ground and tried to use it as shelter. In big, loud letters, the poster advertised: "THE LOST SHRINE OF ZAGAWA — THE EIGHTH WONDER OF THE WORLD!"

Ted watched as the monkey gathered his fallen leaves into a big pile — a pile big enough for two. The monkey nestled under the leaves, out of the rain. Meanwhile the distressing Zagawa poster had mercifully dissolved and Ted was completely exposed to the elements.

Relinquishing his pride, Ted walked over to the monkey. "Oh, no, no, no," he said. "Don't look so satisfied with yourself. The whole reason we're sleeping out here is because of you." Ted lay down next to him. "Yeah, I could be in my nice, warm bed right now, showered, teeth brushed, instead of sleeping out in the cold . . . with a monkey" — he looked up to see the clouds slowly parting. He took in the beautiful, star-filled sky — "under the stars. Wow. Those glow-in-the-dark star stickers have nothing on this."

A firefly darted past their noses and the little monkey pointed excitedly.

"That? That's a firefly," said Ted.

The monkey caught it in his hand and looked it over. Zip, zip. He caught another and then another.

"Oooh, nice grab," cheered Ted.

The monkey gazed in wonder at the winking, blinking cold fire in his hands.

"They're bioluminescent," explained Ted. "Did you know that fireflies glow to remind us —"

The monkey suddenly popped all the fireflies in his mouth at once.

"— uh, that they taste bitter," Ted continued, staring at the monkey in amazement. "It's a defense mechanism."

Gack! They were incredibly yucky! The hungry monkey wanted to swallow them, but he just couldn't. *Ptooy!* He spit them out.

Ted cracked up. "Yeah. Ha, ha! I told you!"

The monkey caught another handful of bugs and offered them to Ted.

"Uh . . . no, no, no. No, thanks. I'm good."

The monkey offered again.

"Yup, you know, there's no way I'm going to eat those bugs, so quit tryin'."

Frustrated, the monkey pushed the whole handful into Ted's mouth.

"Ptooy! Wow. That tastes bad, definitely bitter." He waggled his tongue out of his mouth.

The monkey waggled his tongue and laughed. It was the funniest thing he had ever seen. Both of them had glowing tongues!

"Okay, oh, lishen to thish," Ted lisped with his tongue still hanging out. "I've got a good joke for you. What's the difference between Neanderthal man and Cro-Magnon man?" Ted grinned happily in anticipation of his punch line. "Linguistic competence and polychromatic cave paintings!" he cried, cracking himself up. "You get it? Because . . ."

But the little monkey had cuddled up next to him and fallen fast asleep.

"Hello? You're missing the best part," said Ted.

But the sleeping monkey just snuggled closer.

"Oh, well." Ted sighed. "I need some fresh museum-related material. People depend on me for those jokes."

He lay back in the soft leaves and gazed up at the stars, enjoying the view and, for the moment, blissfully forgetting all his troubles.

The Big Balloon Ride

Early the next morning, the monkey awoke to the sound of children's voices. He followed the sound and came to the entrance of a small zoo. The pretty wrought-iron gate was decorated with big bunches of colorful balloons. The monkey wanted to go in, but he hesitated. Should he leave the man in the yellow hat? The monkey's curiosity was too great and he left the man still sound asleep.

"Oh, no . . . no . . . no. Those are dinosaur bones," murmured Ted in his sleep. "You can't park there. No . . . no . . . there's no parking here. That's my office!" He bolted up from his leafy bed, wide-awake, his heart pounding.

"Whew. It was just a bad dream." He took a deep breath and looked around for the monkey, but he was gone.

"Monkey? Monkey?" he called. "Where are you?"

All of a sudden Ted heard shrieks in the distance. "Oh, no," he groaned. What had the monkey done now? He hurried toward the commotion.

By the time Ted arrived, there was a long line at the zoo's entrance. He had no money for a ticket anyway. So he crept along the fence and found a good place to climb up. From the fencetop, the igloo in the penguin exhibit made the perfect steppingstone in. One big leap and — whoops! He teetered on the slippery dome and tumbled down through the hatch, into the penguins' icy water. A crowd of zoogoers gathered to watch the strange man in yellow surrounded by frolicking penguins.

"Oh, that's cold. It's so much colder than you think." Ted shivered. "I suggest never doing that again, ever. Don't ever swim with penguins; swim with dolphins," he advised the surprised onlookers.

"Hey! Monkey! Monkey!" he heard the children shouting gleefully. He looked around, and there was the monkey, chasing after the kids and trying to grab their balloons.

Ted realized that it was the very same group of students who came regularly to the museum with Miss Dunlop. And for once it didn't look like another disaster — it appeared they were having fun. Ted sighed in relief.

"Oh, Ted. Hi!" called Maggie.

"Miss Maggie," Ted greeted her, tipping his hat politely. Buckets of water poured out on his shoes. The monkey jumped up and down joyfully at the sight of him.

"What happened to you?" asked Maggie.

"Oh, didn't it rain here?" asked Ted nonchalantly.

"Nope, not here," said Maggie.

"Wow, that's crazy," said Ted. "Freak cloudburst down the street."

Suddenly the monkey was perched on Ted's shoulder and his face was smooshed against a big bouquet of balloons. "Please tell me you paid for these," he begged.

"So, how long have you had a monkey?" asked Maggie.

"I don't. I mean, I do. I really don't. Long story." He sighed.

"Hey, mister, what's your monkey's name?" asked one of the kids.

"He doesn't have a name," said Ted.

"He *has* to have a name!" cried another kid.

"Let's give him a name!" they all shouted.

"Please don't . . ." said Ted.

But they ignored him. "How about Fred?" "Jojo!" "Hercules!" "Bananas!" "Dr. Death!" "Elvis!" "Zippy!" "Chelsea!" "Juan Carlos!"

Maggie laughed.

One of the zoo's signs caught Ted's eye: "GEORGE WASHINGTON ZOO."

"Okay, you know what, his name's Washington," said Ted.

"That's a dumb name!" cried one of the kids.

"Then call him *George.* How's that? Happy now?"

They thought about it for a second. The name sounded just right. "George! George!" everyone shouted. "George, here, take my balloon!" "George, come play with me!"

Pretty soon George had such a collection of balloons, he began to hover a couple of inches off the ground!

But Ted didn't notice the new trouble that was brewing. He was thinking about losing his apartment and job; he was remembering that it was true. All of it.

"Ted, are you okay?" asked Maggie.

"It's a long story." Ted sighed. "But it looks like the museum is going to close."

"Really?"

"I know how much you love the museum," said Ted.

"I do love the museum, Ted," said Maggie. "But that's not the only reason I go there every week."

"Yeah, I know. Everyone likes the cafeteria food. Gosh, it's so good."

"I've never had the cafeteria food," said Maggie.

"Really?" asked Ted.

"Really," said Maggie.

Was that a twinkle in her eye? Ted wondered. How could he have been so oblivious? She was adorable!

He gazed into her eyes. "So, you've never had the tuna hash on Thursday?"

"Never." She gazed back.

"It's really quite something."

"I'll remember that," she said.

"There's also a meatless meatloaf on Monday which is . . . quite special."

"Quite special," agreed Maggie, hanging on his every word.

One of the kids tugged at Ted's pant leg, pleading, "You have to help George!" But all Ted could see at that moment was Maggie.

The kid poked him. "George needs you!" he repeated.

"Take a message," said Ted. "I'm busy."

"He has an emergency!"

“The restrooms are behind the penguin habitat,” said Ted, his eyes still fixed on Maggie.

“Mister! Your monkey is floating away!”

The kids were jumping up and down and pointing. Ted looked. George was ten feet in the air and moving fast. Everyone ran to keep up.

“Hey, monkey! Don’t be afraid!” called Ted. “Just keep your head together and don’t look down!”

George looked down. A look of pure terror washed over his face.

“Help him, Mister! Help him! You gotta save George!” cried the kids.

“Who, me?” asked Ted.

“Yes, you!” they all cried.

“’Kay . . .” Ted hesitated, wondering what in the world he was supposed to do.

“Hurry, Ted. He’s floating away!” cried Maggie.

Ted noticed the balloon man’s cart with its bunch of balloons. That bunch was three times the size of George’s! “I’m commandeering those balloons,” he declared as he grabbed the whole bunch. He ran and leapt into the air like a ballet dancer.

"Hey! Hey! Where you going? Come back here!" shouted the balloon seller.

But Ted couldn't get off the ground. He needed even more balloons, and fast. The kids handed over all that were left. It was just the lift he needed.

"Here I goooooooo. . . ." He floated over the alligator pit. Too low! The alligators snapped at his toes. "Ooh, oh, oh!" He pulled his legs up against his chest.

"Boy, glad that's over." He sighed, just in time to drift slowly down . . . into the lions' den exhibit. "Aaaugh!" Ted pushed off the ground and launched himself up again. Higher and higher . . . he floated away from the hungry cats.

But way above him, little George was starting to panic. He clung to his balloon strings for dear life.

"Hang on, little fella, I'm coming!" shouted Ted. He followed George over the zoo's walkway.

Still, Ted didn't have enough lift to catch up with George. "I gotta borrow those," he cried, snatching balloons from everyone on the way. "I need these. Official zoo business."

George floated through a forest of giraffe heads.

"Wait for me, monkey!" called Ted.

He crashed into one spotted head after another. "Excuse me. I'm sorry. My fault." He cringed, leaving the poor giraffes with their necks in a tangle.

Higher and higher Ted pursued George — over the zoo fence and out over the park. Ted realized he needed more momentum if he was ever going to catch up. He spotted a kid flying a kite. That might work!

"Sorry, I need this," he cried as he swooped and grabbed the string out of the kid's hand. "How do you steer these things?"

The kite took a nosedive, pulling Ted down and then up again like a roller coaster. "Hang on, George, I'm coming!" he shouted.

But George kept on floating — over the tops of the skyscrapers, over the city traffic, over the baseball stadium.

"It's a home run!" shouted the announcer.

The crowd roared.

Thwap! The ball bounced off Ted's leg and shot back down into the stadium, where it fell smack into the right fielder's glove.

The crowd groaned.

"Third out," cried the announcer. "The curse continues. . . ."

Ted didn't have time to worry about the game. George was headed for some dangerous antipigeon spikes on top of a skyscraper. “Monkey! Monkey! Watch out!” he cried.

George’s balloons began to pop against the sharp points. Suddenly he was plummeting to the ground!

“George! George! Whoa!” cried Ted. Just in time he swooped down like Spiderman and caught the monkey midfall. “Gotcha! Wow.” Ted sighed with relief as George climbed up his arm and clutched him tight. The monkey whimpered with fear.

“You’re safe now, George. I’ve got you.” Ted rubbed the little monkey’s back. “It’s okay, George. Hey, I like that name. It suits you.”

George buried his face in Ted’s shoulder. He was afraid to look down.

“Actually, this isn’t too bad,” Ted said. “I can’t believe I’m doing this. This is awesome.”

Finally George peeked out with one eye. He took in the full view. He was flying with his best friend and it *was* awesome! Ted let him take charge of steering with the kite string. They drifted over the big bridge and the ships in the harbor. They sailed along with the birds and the clouds.

“Look, George, there’s the museum.” Ted pointed. “All those people down there are waiting to see this.” He pulled the idol out of his pocket. “Hey, folks! Here it is! Here’s the idol!”

Held out at arm's length against the background of the city, the idol really did seem huge. "If only I could make it look that big." Ted sighed. "Wait. *I* can't, but maybe Clovis can! Okay, George, hand me that pink balloon . . . and hang on!"

George handed Ted the blue balloon.

"Close enough!" Ted untied the balloon's string and used the jet of escaping helium to propel them to Clovis's loft apartment.

The Magnificator

Clovis was busy in his laboratory examining a popcorn kernel under a magnifying device when he heard a loud crash. He looked up and saw Ted and George floating down onto his balcony.

"Huh? Oh, I predicted this. Balloon travel finally coming back into fashion," said Clovis.

"Clovis, I've got a problem," said Ted, climbing through the open window.

Clovis put on his glasses and peered at the little brown furball by Ted's side. "Wait just a minute. Are you returning him?" he demanded.

"What?" asked Ted.

"I have a strict no-return policy on any robotic animals I create," explained Clovis, "unless you have a receipt." He whipped out his magnifying glass and studied George closely.

"No, Clovis. Calm down," said Ted. "This is George. He's a real monkey."

"Oh, well, then . . ." Clovis introduced George to his robotic dog, Sparky, and turned his attention back to his popcorn experiment.

"I really need your help," said Ted. He dug the little idol out of his pocket. "Here's my problem."

Clovis pulled his "GAGA FOR ZAGAWA" key chain out of his pocket and compared. "Yes, I see. You're just missing the chain. I think I have an extra —"

"No, Clovis. This is the *idol.*"

"I'm not one to judge," said Clovis, "but haven't you exaggerated its size just a little?"

Clovis clapped his hands and a big robotic penguin appeared. "This is Frosty," he said, opening a door on the front of the penguin and pulling out a stick of butter.

"Thanks, Frosty."

Clovis unwrapped the butter and put it on top of a bag of popcorn kernels.

"What's that?" asked Ted.

"Um, nothing," said Clovis. He pulled a pair of goggles down over Ted's eyes.

"Should I be concerned?" asked Ted.

"No . . ." said Clovis, gesturing to a padded wall, "not if you're behind that." He wound up a cuckoo clock and set it inside a big metal container. "Fire in the hole!" he shouted.

"George! Look out!" warned Ted.

The clock ticked. Clovis and Ted dove behind the blast shield.

Ding! Cuckoo!

BOOM!

George and Sparky jumped into each other's arms.

As the smoke cleared, Ted saw a mountain of white puffy stuff in the middle of the floor. "Is that popcorn?"

"I call it boomcorn," said Clovis. "It's for really big sleepovers with a lot of kids." He sampled one of the softball-size kernels. "Hmm. Not quite right." He spit it out, and BANG! — the wastebasket burst into flames.

Clovis snapped his fingers to call Soaky, the robotic elephant, who promptly put the fire out with his fire-hose trunk.

"All right, let's see what we can do with that key chain," said Clovis.

"Idol," Ted corrected him.

"Idol, right. Yes," he said, throwing the tarps off various

machines and considering each one in turn. "I can make it a different color, I can make it light up, I can make it into a piggy bank. . . ."

"Can you make it into a four-story piggy bank?"

While the men were discussing the machines, George was having a wonderful time exploring the laboratory with Sparky and Soaky. He discovered Clovis's magnifying glass and began peering through it like Sherlock Holmes.

George spied a spider crawling on the floor. It looked so cute, he wanted to keep it. He found an empty snow globe and set it down over the spider. The spider grew larger. George took the snow globe off and the spider went back to being small. George wanted a big spider. He put the snow globe over it again. Sparky helped George pile on more snow globes. The spider grew bigger and bigger. What fun!

Clovis considered his snow-globe-making machine. "I could make it into a snow globe — with real snow," he told Ted.

"Clovis, focus!" cried Ted.

"Right — *bigger,* like . . . that?" Clovis gaped at the huge image that had just appeared on the wall behind Ted.

Ted turned and saw a monstrous ten-foot-tall spider! "Argggh!" He darted behind Clovis for protection.

"Do you see a very big spider?" asked Clovis.

Sparky barked and pointed to George, standing on the overhead projector next to his pile of snow globes.

"George, did you do this?" demanded Clovis.

George nodded sheepishly.

"Don't get mad at him," said Ted.

"Mad, no!" cried Clovis. "I think he may have the answer to your problem."

"Awesome. Good work, George!" cried Ted. "Clovis, I need to borrow your truck. And the magnification machine."

"Sure. Wait, wait — who's going to drive? You or George?"

Ted gave him a look.

Clovis pulled out the truck key on its "GAGA FOR ZAGAWA" key chain and handed it over to Ted.

"Thanks, Clove!"

"Be careful! It's a classic!" shouted Clovis as Ted and George zoomed off to the museum.

Gridlock

When Mr. Bloomsberry arrived at the museum that day, he couldn't believe his eyes. People were lined up around the block, waiting to see the new exhibit.

He hurried to Junior's office. "I don't understand. I thought I told you to cancel the exhibit," he said.

"Me? I don't think so, because I would have done it," replied Junior, sipping his coffee. "No, this has the look of Ted on it. Yes, Ted is the one we're mad at for this."

Bloomsberry's phone rang. "Hello?"

"Hello, Mr. Bloomsberry. Ted here."

"Ted. Ted? Are you serious?" asked Bloomsberry.

"No — I mean, no, sir. I . . . don't hang up . . . !"

"Ted, I don't have time for this."

"I know!" cried Ted. "I have the solution!"

“Solution? Solution to what?”

“The exhibit can open as planned.”

“How is that possible?”

“I’ll explain it when I see you,” said Ted. “All you need to know is that the *Eagle* has landed.”

“Eagle?” asked Bloomsberry. “What eagle?”

“No, no, the idol would be the eagle.”

Mr. Bloomsberry was more confused than ever.

“You know what? It’s not a big deal,” said Ted. “Don’t worry about it. I’ll be there in fifteen minutes!”

Meanwhile the curious monkey couldn’t wait to try the new invention again. Such interesting buttons and levers! He crawled through the truck’s rear window and hopped into the cargo bed. His foot pressed on the special magnification dial Clovis had designed. He pulled the projection lever, peered into the lens, and brushed the scan button with his other foot. Wow! He looked up and saw a giant 3-D, five-story monkey just down the street. He scratched his head, puzzled. The big monkey scratched his head too. The small monkey made scary faces and waved his arms out like a monster. So did the big monkey.

Pedestrians stopped in the crosswalks. Traffic screeched to a halt. Everywhere people were screaming and fleeing for their lives.

Ted drove on, oblivious to the King Kong effect the little monkey was having on the terrified city.

"This gridlock," he fumed. "What's going on out there?"

He saw the horrified look on the face of an oncoming driver. The driver was looking up in the air! He swerved this way and that. Ted veered off to avoid a collision. "Hold on, George!" he shouted. The little monkey fell from his perch on the projector. Ted checked his rearview mirror and all he saw behind him was wreckage.

"I'm seeing multiple violations of the rules of the road. Multiple violations!" he cried.

He zigzagged through the stalled cars, determined to get their new invention to the museum.

George climbed back up onto the projector.

A passing cab driver glanced at the huge monkey in the sky.

"Oh, yeah. A forty-foot monkey. Seen that. It's always something," said the cynical cabbie to the shocked tourists in the back seat.

"Is that the same monkey who ruined my apartment?" sang Ms. Plushbottom from the back of her limousine as it too tried to pass through the busy streets.

Eeeerrrkkk! Crash! Her chauffeur slammed on the brakes and plowed into the back of a paint truck. A rainbow of colors came pouring in through her sunroof.

Yes, that would be the same monkey, Ms. Plushbottom decided.

"This traffic is crazy," cried Ted. "I'm going to get off Broadway and try Sixth Avenue."

Ted shouted at a driver who was coming down the ramp on the wrong side. "That does it! There are lines painted on the street for a reason! George, take down that license-plate number!"

Why was the man yelling for George? The monkey wanted to know. He climbed down from the projector and scooted back into the front seat. Ted glanced over at him for the first time. "George, what are you thinking?" he cried. "Put on your seat belt! Every nut case in the city is on the road today."

Sabotage!

Ted and George finally pulled up at the museum's loading dock. Everywhere they looked the streets were jammed with cars.

"Wow. I guess there *is* a parking problem in this city." Ted whistled. They carried their invention into the museum and Ted set it on an empty hot-dog cart.

Mr. Bloomsberry and his son were in the exhibit room looking out the window at the thousands of patrons waiting to buy their tickets.

"You know, Father, when I see a crowd like that I have to ask, where did they all park? Because that's where the real money is," said Junior, sipping his latte.

"Mr. Bloomsberry! Mr. Bloomsberry!" Ted called.

They turned to see Ted rolling the squeaky hot-dog cart down the hall toward them. The havoc-wreaking monkey stood on the front of the cart like a heroic hood ornament.

"Oh, no!" cried Junior. "No, no, no. That's it. Get that little jungle thing out of here before he destroys something else."

"Hold on there, son," said Bloomsberry. "Ted, what is this contraption?"

"Stand back, everyone, and prepare to be amazed," declared Ted. "Here, George. Let's show 'em our magnificator!"

Ted held out the monkey statuette: "Small idol."

He flipped the switch on the magnificator. Its scanning light hummed and it projected a huge, forty-foot-tall, 3-D Zagawa idol onto the stage.

"Big idol!" cried Ted triumphantly. "Isn't it awesome?"

Mr. Bloomsberry was enthralled. "I see. We optically enlarge the statue." He put his hand in front of the magnifying lens and a giant projection of his hand appeared next to the idol.

"Yes. I see. I suppose this might work. Yes . . . this will definitely work."

"Well, sir," said Ted, "the credit really should go to George. . . ."

But Junior was far from convinced. "Excuse me. Hello. Voice of reason. Like to introduce myself. . . . Are we so desperate that we'll lie to our public?"

"Nonsense," said Mr. Bloomsberry. "We promised those

people something awe inspiring, and we're giving it to them — thanks to Ted and George." He put his arm around Ted affectionately. "I knew you wouldn't let me down."

"Well, sir, I gotta tell you, I came pretty close," confessed Ted.

"No, no, Ted, I'm so proud of you," said Bloomsberry. "You're like the son I never had."

Junior nearly choked on his latte. "Father, I'm your son, remember?"

"Yes, but I *had* you," he replied. "Ted, this is amazing."

"Yes, of course. What was I thinking?" Junior fumed.

While Ted and his father were admiring the realistic image, Junior poured half his latte into the projector's cooling vent.

George watched him, curious.

"Hey, monkey want a sip? Go on, take it. Yummy. Creamy. Mmmm, yes, good . . ." Junior coaxed.

George grabbed the cup and took a drink. Mmmm, yummy!

While the monkey sipped, Junior put his arms around Ted's and his father's shoulders and pretended to admire the idol along with them. "I guess the world didn't need another parking lot after all. Hey, you did it! Another great Ted moment!"

"Thank you," said Ted.

"We've got nobody to thank but you," said Junior.

As they watched, the projected idol crackled and zipped and then POOF! — it was gone.

"Burp."

Ted and Mr. Bloomsberry spun around to see the little monkey on the projector, with a latte mustache.

BOOM! The projector exploded, sending George crashing to the floor in a pile of rubble. The magnificator was wrecked.

"George, what did you do?" cried Ted.

George shook his head.

"Oh, Ted," said Junior. "I warned you about that monkey."

"You don't give a monkey coffee!" exclaimed Ted.

George was confused. What were the people yelling about?

Junior went into a smug, self-satisfied tirade. He pointed at the cowering monkey. "And now he's gone and destroyed the last chance we had of saving my father's museum. It's my father's only museum. What have you done, Ted, what have you done?" Junior made a *tsk-tsk* sound.

"What was I thinking?" Mr. Bloomsberry sighed. "We've just been fooling ourselves. It's over."

"But, sir, I still think we could . . ." Ted began. But Junior was already escorting his father out of the exhibit room.

"Ted, I said it's over," said Mr. Bloomsberry, defeated.

"It's okay, Father," consoled Junior. "I'm here. Your son, your real son, Junior — not Ted. Yes, Father, we'll be fine."

Ted looked down at George. The little monkey smiled and offered him the last sip of latte.

Animal Control

It was time to face the crowd outside the museum. Ted knew he couldn't delay it any longer. He walked to the front door and took a deep breath. George tried to follow.

"No, no, George," said Ted. "You just stay here."

As he swung the door open, he spotted Maggie with her schoolchildren among the sea of faces. He swallowed hard.

"Excuse me. Uh, I-I'm . . ." he stammered.

The exasperated crowd turned their eyes to him, waiting for some explanation for the long delay.

"I'm sorry, everybody. The museum's closed," he announced.

"For how long?" asked a girl.

"Forever," replied Ted.

"But I want to see the giant idol!" someone cried.

"There never was one. It was all a big mistake," said Ted.

The crowd grumbled and noisily dispersed. Maggie herded

her schoolkids back onto their bus. When they were safely aboard, she went over to Ted and smiled sympathetically. "I'm so sorry."

The school-bus driver honked for her. She patted Ted's shoulder. "I have to go now. I'll be back."

Ted sat forlornly on the museum steps.

George didn't understand why the man was so glum. He climbed into Ted's lap and smiled.

"It's too late to cheer me up," grumbled Ted. "You think life's just nonstop fun and games, don't you? Well, it's not, George. At least not for me."

George put Ted's hat on and tried a game of peekaboo.

But the man wasn't in the mood. "George, please just leave me alone. You're better off without me."

George shook his little head in disagreement.

"This is not good — you and me," Ted continued. "You belong in the jungle. I belong . . . somewhere without a monkey. I don't want — I *can't* have you in my life."

George smiled and hopped up on Ted's arm.

"No," said Ted. He shook George off and rose to return to the museum.

George began to follow him up the steps.

“Look, monkey, don’t follow me!” Ted commanded.

The monkey dropped back, finally getting the idea.

Ted was about to go back into the museum when the animal-control truck skidded to a stop outside the museum steps. Two officers circled around George and threw a net over him. “Gotcha! All right, now, take it easy, little fella. Easy. Easy.”

Ted advanced toward the officers. “Hey, not so rough!” he called out.

“Stand back,” said one of the officers. “I know he looks cute, but this one’s supposed to have teeth like Ginsu knives.”

George slipped away from them and grabbed Ted’s leg.

“Guys. Could you just take him? Please. And don’t hurt him,” said Ted.

The officer removed the monkey from Ted’s leg. “Relax, little fella,” said the officer. “Back to Africa with you.” He put George in a small cage, locked the door, and loaded him onto the back of the truck. The officers planned to drive poor George to the docks and put him on the next ship to Africa.

Ted couldn’t watch. He turned and walked up the stairs. He heard the back door of the truck slam shut and he groaned as if he’d been punched hard in the stomach. The truck left.

"Turn Your Eye to the Light . . ."

Ted couldn't bear to go back to the museum. For hours he walked the streets, dejected. Everything reminded him of his little friend. He caught his own reflection in the safari outfitter's window and lifted his hat up and down nostalgically.

"Peekaboo, peekaboo," he said to the window. "Ahhh, George, he loved peekaboo."

A girl with a red balloon reminded him of his amazing balloon ride over the city with George.

Outside an apartment building, an open bucket of yellow paint reminded him of George's artwork. "He loved primary colors," he sighed absent-mindedly. He dipped his hand in the bucket and made yellow handprints along the side of the building.

"Hey, hey!" shouted the painter, waving angrily at Ted to stop.

Ted looked up. The painter slipped and was dangling upside down, his foot caught between two rungs of the ladder.

Ted chuckled to himself, remembering his trip down the fire escape with George. Suddenly he spotted a similar monkey across the street!

"George! How did you get out?" he cried.

He dashed across, snarling traffic in both directions. He pushed through the crowd on the sidewalk . . . but it wasn't George. It was George on an eight-foot plasma television screen in the window of TV World. The news anchorperson was talking about the giant monkey that had terrorized the city earlier in the day.

"That's why the traffic was so bad," said Ted. "Oh, George."

They showed footage of cars piled up and people screaming and running in all directions.

Ted sighed again. "Those were some good times. We had some fun, didn't we?"

As he rounded the corner, Ted ran into a man in a monkey costume handing out coupons. The man offered Ted one, but Ted didn't take it. Instead he gazed at him, teary-eyed, and gave him a big hug.

The man didn't know what to do. "Uh, sir —" he began.

Maggie came around the corner. "Ted, I've been looking for you," she said.

Ted stared at her over the shoulder of the monkey man.

"Is . . . is everything okay?" she asked.

"Yeah. Sure. Why?"

"Well, you *are* hugging a man dressed in a monkey costume."

Ted pulled himself together and let the man go. "And . . . good luck with that, Phil. Great to see you again," he said, pretending to know the man in the suit.

Maggie suggested a little walk in the park. As they strolled, Ted told her the whole sad story.

"So after they took him away, I've been wandering the streets, and you saw me hugging a man in a monkey suit. That pretty much catches you up. I can't believe George is gone, and it's all my fault," lamented Ted.

"Yes, it is," agreed Maggie.

"What?" asked Ted, surprised by her bluntness.

"The question is — what are you going to do about it?"

Ted straightened up and looked Maggie in the eye. "You're right, it *is* my fault," he declared. "Now, if you'll excuse me, I have a date with a monkey." He dashed off purposefully.

In a second he was back. "You know, I don't have a date with a monkey. It was just my way of saying that I'm going after George," he explained.

"Ted," said Maggie firmly, waving him away.

"Right. Bye!"

In the harbor, the ship to Africa was taking on its final load. George's cage sat in a lonely little corner of the cargo hold amid the piles of steamer trunks and wooden crates. A sailor slammed the hatch shut and George slumped back in his cage.

Ted could hear the ship's low horn sounding as he sped toward the dock in Clovis's classic pickup truck. The ship was about to depart! Ted could see it slowly pulling away from the dock.

"Oh, no. I'm too late," he moaned. "Or am I?"

Ted had an idea. He tightened his seat belt. "Luckily, movies have taught me exactly what to do in this situation." He down-shifted and drove full throttle toward the pier.

"Kids, don't try this at home . . . !"

He shifted into high gear and floored it. The truck rocketed down the pier and launched into the air, out across the water . . .

"What am I doing?" cried Ted. "This isn't a movie. It's real! AAAAAAAAAHHHHHHHHHH!"

The truck began its descent. . . . It was going to make it! Yes!

Ted closed his eyes. *Kersplash!*

"Oh, no . . ."

Ted opened his eyes. The truck had nose-dived into a swimming pool. A group of senior citizens dressed up in tuxedos and gowns and holding fancy drinks stared at him speechlessly.

"This is odd," said Ted. "You guys are a little dressed up for a cargo ship to Africa, don't you think?"

The cargo ship's horn sounded its low blast again. Suddenly Ted realized he wasn't on the cargo ship. He was on a cruise ship! The ship to Africa was pulling out alongside them.

"Ah, excuse me," Ted apologized to the people in their soaking dress-up clothes.

"I'm coming for you!" he shouted across the water to George. He dove into the harbor and swam with all his might.

He reached the ship's anchor just as it was being hoisted out of the water. The anchor swung back and forth in front of one of the portholes like a pendulum.

"George! George!" called Ted. He maneuvered the anchor so one of the tips was aimed straight at the porthole, and he used it like a battering ram to crash through the glass. Ted climbed through the porthole and jumped down into the cargo hold.

"George!" he called.

George didn't hear him. He was curled up in his little cage, lonely and depressed. A rat peered in at him through the bars, but George didn't care. The rat swiped his banana and scurried away.

Ted searched the dark, cavernous hold, calling out to keep his courage up. "George? Are you here? I *think* you're here. George?"

Finally the little monkey raised his head. Was that a familiar voice he heard? He stood up and began making excited monkey noises.

Ted leapt over a crate. "There you are!" he cried.

George rattled the bars of his cage in glee.

Ted wondered how to break the lock. He looked around and spotted a fire extinguisher. Regarding it doubtfully, Ted pried it off the wall.

"Stand back, buddy!" he told George. He lifted it over his head and slammed it down on the lock. The lock sprang open. Not bad, thought Ted.

"George, give me a hug, you little furball!"

George leapt into Ted's arms and ruffled his hair.

"There, there. You're all right," said Ted. "I'm so sorry. I don't know how I let them take you away."

Ted took the idol out of his pocket and set it on top of George's cage. "This was so important to me, but somehow it just doesn't matter anymore. What matters is you and me, George. Our buddyship."

George was very happy to see Ted too, but he was also curious about the pretty pattern that suddenly appeared on the side of the crate behind Ted. A shaft of moonlight from the porthole shone right through the tiny holes in the idol, and it was projecting a familiar design. It was the same half circle with little circles around it that had been carved into the alcove where the idol had been found in the jungle.

"Now we can do all the monkey things we've always wanted to do. I'll get an organ and a grind, and you can dance for money," gushed Ted. "Or . . . or . . . *I* can dance for money. Who knows. We'll figure it out. We can take turns."

But George just jumped up and down excitedly, pointing at the crate.

"George, do you mind?" fussed Ted. "I'm expressing some feelings here. It's kind of hard, okay? Now, where was I . . . right . . . who's going to dance? No, no — adventure! You brought adventure into my life. . . ."

George grabbed Ted's head, braced his feet on his shoulders, and twisted him so he was facing the projected image. He held his paws against Ted's lips to get him to stop talking and *look.*

"An now you know that'sh all that mattersh . . ." Ted was saying between squished lips as he turned. At last he saw the projected image.

"Wait!" he cried. He recognized the design. "Wait! Where's that coming from? It's a pictogram. George, it's a map! We had it all along."

He stepped up to get a closer look. "Of course. 'Turn your eye to the light . . .'" he said, remembering the words of the inscription, " 'go from blindness to sight.' I was supposed to hold the statue up to the light!"

Ted had an idea. "George!" he cried. "Pack your things — we're off to Africa on the very next ship!"

George looked confused. The ship's horn sounded again.

"Wait a minute — we're already on a ship to Africa!" cried Ted. "Man, what a timesaver."

Romancing the Idol

Reunited with Edu and his porters and equipped with the secret map of light, Ted and George soon discovered the location of the Lost Shrine of Zagawa. They knew just what to do with it.

It took a few weeks and ten pairs of elephants to haul the immense idol through the jungle to the ship and, once at their final destination, down the city streets toward the Oswald J. Bloomsberry Museum. All along the sidewalks, people stopped and stared. Never had they seen anything like it. Ted and George rode atop the crated shrine, waving like the grand marshals of their own parade.

Old Mr. Bloomsberry, who had never really lost faith in Ted was beside himself with delight. "Ted's back!" he cried, dashing out the front door of his museum to greet the returning adventurers.

Junior trailed behind him, sipping his usual cup of coffee.

"Ooh, Ted's back," he muttered. "All right, well, let's see what the great Ted has done now."

When he saw the immense idol in its crate standing outside the museum steps, Junior froze in his tracks. "Oh, you've got to be kidding . . ." he moaned. The door swung back and slapped against the coffee cup in his hand. "Ow, ow, ow!" he cried, trying to mop up the hot liquid that had spilled on him.

"Mr. Bloomsberry!" Ted and George waved to him triumphantly.

The crowd cheered, and Ted invited everyone to attend the grand opening the next week.

When the grand opening of the exhibit rolled around, streamers, balloons, and banners with the slogan "IT'S HERE!" decorated the museum. People from all over the city gathered to buy their tickets.

Ms. Plushbottom pulled up in her limo. Her chauffeur got out and waited for the museum's new parking valet — Bloomsberry junior! When he appeared around the corner in his cheap tuxedo uniform, the chauffeur tossed him the keys.

"We've been waiting," Ms. Plushbottom huffed.

Junior was sweaty and out of breath. "Sorry, the nearest parking lot is . . . five blocks away."

"I know. I own the parking lot," said Ms. Plushbottom. "That's where the real money is," she added.

"That's my line," groaned Junior.

When the eager crowd had assembled in the big exhibit room, Ted dimmed the lights. Dramatic music began playing, and a thick fog rolled across the stage. "Ladies and gentlemen," said the recorded voice, "the Bloomsberry Museum is proud to finally bring you . . . the eighth wonder of the world: the Lost Shrine of Zagawa!"

Colorful laser lights crisscrossed the stage as Ted slowly pulled the cover from the shrine.

The audience went wild.

"Okay, now *that* I haven't seen," declared the cynical cabbie.

Ted stepped up to the podium. He shuffled a big stack of note cards. Maggie's kids cringed. Not more lecture notes!

"As I stand in front of the Lost Shrine of Zagawa . . . " he began.

Uh, oh, thought Maggie. She hoped he did not have one of his long lectures planned.

"I just have one important thing to say. Anyone can memorize facts and figures. The real way to learn anything is to go out and experience it and let your curiosity lead you." He tossed his note cards away and smiled at Maggie. She smiled back at him, and George jumped into his arms.

"So, who's ready to learn?" he cried.

Another cheer. The kids moved forward to get a closer look at the idol. Maggie unhooked the velvet ropes, motioning for the kids to come in.

"Come on. Come on," Ted encouraged them. Clearly this was a newer, more permissive and engaging Ted. Having a monkey had been good for him. The kids jostled each other in delight at the chance to be the first to get an up-close view of the giant statue.

Next door to the main exhibit was the brand-new Paint Like George Room. All the adults hurried there first.

In the painting area, everyone donned yellow smocks, dipped their hands into cans of paint, and made handprints on a huge canvas.

"Oh, this is so exhilarating!" sang Ms. Plushbottom. "You know, I have an original 'George' in my penthouse."

Ted saw George painting a monkey on the back of a big, burly man's shirt.

"Good work, George."

The man turned around. It was Ivan!

"Hey!" he cried.

Yikes! Ted ducked into the crowd. He was making his way toward Maggie when that familiar booming voice made him jump again.

"There you are, Seventeen B!"

"Boy, you're light on your feet for a big man," said Ted.

"Ivan change building policy from no pet to pet. Ivan like pets now."

"Oh, that's great, Ivan," Ted said with feeling.

George jumped up on Ivan's shoulder, leaving two red palm prints on Ivan's cheeks.

"Georgie, you get so cute," said Ivan. "I think he likes me."

On the other side of the Paint Like George Room, kids were climbing a rock wall. George hopped down and hurried over to show them how to do it monkey-style.

Over in the magnificator demonstration zone, kids took

turns waiting for Clovis to project gigantic images of each of them on the wall.

"Say, have you seen Sparky?" asked Clovis.

"I found a femur!" shouted one of the kids in the fossil excavation section.

"I found Sparky!" cried another kid, pulling the little robot out of the sand.

The entire exhibit was a huge hit. Another of Clovis's robots, Soaky, was helping the balloon man inflate balloons with helium. George wanted to help too! He handed balloons out to a line of kids — one, two, three. Oops! One balloon slipped out of his grasp.

George ran after it, up the stairs and outside across a narrow walkway. There, standing upright in front of him, was a huge rocket ship.

It was an impressive sight to the small monkey. George looked it over eagerly. What was that shiny red button in the cockpit? The monkey was definitely curious.

In the lobby Ted and Mr. Bloomsberry were finishing up their successful press conference. Every major TV network and newspaper had sent its reporters to cover the Zagawa story — after checking that it was real this time, of course.

"All right, all right, last question," said Bloomsberry, a little hoarse from the interview.

"Ted, where will you and George go for your next adventure?" asked one of the reporters. "The Arctic? South America? Egypt?"

Ted saw Maggie in the crowd and smiled. He went over to her and put his arm around her. "You know, you don't need to go around the world for a great adventure." He gazed into Maggie's eyes. "I have a lot of things to catch up on right here."

"Really?" asked Maggie, enchanted.

"Really," said Ted.

He was about to lean over and kiss her when one of the kids gave his pant leg a tug. "Mister, mister, George is —"

"I know, he's cute and lovable," said Ted.

"Very cute, very lovable." Maggie sighed, still looking into Ted's eyes.

"Yeah, well, he's also in that rocket!" shouted the kids.

"It's okay, there's no fuel in it," said Ted dreamily.

Suddenly the floor shook as the sound of rocket boosters

whirling to life reverberated throughout the museum.

Ted looked worried. "Clovis, you didn't put fuel in that rocket, did you?"

"Uh, maybe."

Ted raced to the rocket to save George.

Clovis turned to Ivan and shrugged. "I see a rocket with empty fuel tanks, what am I supposed to do?"

"Absolutely," agreed Ivan. "You can't read minds."

Ted scrambled across the walkway. He could see George sitting in the cockpit, smiling. "George, wait!" he cried. He leapt into the cockpit with the little monkey and slammed the canopy closed just as the rocket began to lift off.

"Careful, Ted. Hurry back!" Maggie called after them.

Inside the cockpit, Ted admonished the little monkey. "Okay, once around the Earth and then straight back home. You hear me? Okay? I've got plans tonight."

The rocket raced into orbit. George climbed into Ted's lap. What were all those other buttons for? The monkey wanted to know.

"Gosh, no, no, no, George," cried Ted. "I am not letting you drive. Just sit back and —"

The little monkey reached for the control panel.

"George, don't push that button, I don't know what it does. George . . ."

Suddenly the rocket sped up and zoomed straight out of Earth's orbit.

"Hold on, George!" cried Ted in glee. "Oh, boy, what a surge of adrenaline. I'm going to sleep good tonight!"

The End